Boots
TO
Stilettos

CY Collinsmiller

authorHOUSE®

AuthorHouse™
1663 Liberty Drive
Bloomington, IN 47403
www.authorhouse.com
Phone: 1 (800) 839-8640

Published by AuthorHouse 03/12/2019

ISBN: 978-1-5462-7209-0 (sc)
ISBN: 978-1-5462-7207-6 (hc)
ISBN: 978-1-5462-7208-3 (e)

Library of Congress Control Number: 2018915028

To my children and grandchildren: Life is beautiful! No matter where the paths of life take you, enjoy the journey. Always remember I love you, and God loves you so much more. Keep him first in your life. You are always in my prayers. Stay strong. All is well.

To Jodie Bonham: You have been my greatest supporter and most reliable friend. You have always understood how important writing is to me. I have called on you for so many things, and you never failed to assist. Your support is greatly appreciated; without you, my staying on this course might not have been possible. Thank you, and God bless you always.

To my crew: You left an impression on my heart that will never go away. I often think of you and smile. You made it a joy to come to work each day. We faced many challenges and accomplished each with professionalism and enthusiasm. We made a great team. Thank you, and God's grace be with you.

In Remembrance
Ray
Ruby
Mae-Mae
Lisa
Rahsaan
MyLuv
Bruh-Bruh

Our hearts are still heavy. You all left so suddenly, so tragically. When your names come up in conversations, as they often do, the shock can still be seen on the faces of most, and some shake their heads. Fortunately, the pain of losing you can never outweigh the joy of knowing you. We love and miss you deeply, and you will not be forgotten. May you all rest in peace.

Vengeance Is Mine: The Key to Peace and Freedom from Injustices
Kids Will Be Kids: but Oh My God
Boots to Stilettos: Stepping Out in a New Direction

These books are all introductions to the life of Karah Woodard.

Before Karah turned twenty, she'd already faced many hardships and made decisions that made her life difficult. She grew up in a troubled household, where lack and abuse were overwhelming. At age sixteen, she got pregnant, and the next two years brought two more children. Now with a family of three depending on her, she became more determined than ever before. She was committed to overcoming any obstacle that prevented her from becoming the best mother she could be.

Karah was always compelled to look to the heavens for direction. She'd lost her dad in a boating accident when she was only two years old, and his absence was profound. Her mom told her much he adored his baby girl. She said that after his death, Karah often sat near the door where he normally came into the house. She was accustomed to his coming home from work and showering his love on her. As they sat for dinner, Dad would feed her from his spoon, and she would try to feed him.

After his death, her mother often walked into the kitchen to see Karah sitting there with her spoon extended. At first it was alarming and painful for her mother. It was apparent that she missed Dad. Undoubtedly her young mind was full of confusion. She couldn't speak her thoughts, so she communicated in her own way. Surely, she wanted to know where her daddy was. *Mama said Daddy is in heaven? Where is heaven?* she must have thought. No matter how young she was, those emotions had a psychological effect on the child.

Over the years, a different phenomenon was revealed: She could see him. Karah's dad would appear to her as she lay in bed, staring at the ceiling. He'd always say, "Be a good girl. Daddy's always watching over you." Since she described seeing things in the spiritual realm, elders of the church considered her to have a spirit of discernment.

Nevertheless, Karah learned to identify the difference between God in heaven and that her father was in heaven. She learned that

God was the Creator and ruler of the universe. She learned that God had given his only Son to the world and allowed him to be crucified and to die on the cross so that we could be saved. She also learned that if you wanted to go to heaven, you had to ask his Son, Jesus Christ, to come into your life so he could guide you. Karah believed all that she learned.

At around age eighteen, Karah asked Jesus to come into her life. Once she became a Christian, the forces of Satan, God's enemy, came against her. Karah quickly recognized these tricks of the devil. She always felt she would survive, but Satan's attacks were relentless. Every negative force was trying to bring Karah down.

My three books are a theme-based attempt to categorize what is viewed as Karah's most challenging obstacles. *Vengeance Is Mine* describes issues where hurt and disappointment could have kept Karah entangled, but learning to accept that vengeance belongs to God sets her free.

Kids Will Be Kids tells of a mother's love and passion for her children and the many issues she faces during that process. Then, after fighting many battles and overcoming many obstacles, she has an overwhelming need for peace. She is desperate for peace and prays for peace, but trying to find peace is the hardest thing she has to learn. Life still rages all around her. Her children and grandchildren struggle with life's issues. Then, when her mother dies, she's even more lost and confused. It seems that peace is impossible. Once again, the spirit of God speaks to her. Every sermon she hears and every scripture she reads seem to fill her with the importance of resting in God's peace.

This book, *Boots to Stilettos: Stepping Out in a New Direction*, describes that stage of Karah's life.

1

Maxine's Web

My eyes couldn't stop moving as I traveled slowly through the small house. Up and down, left and right, pictures filled the walls. They all provided a glimpse into the life of my mother, Maxine Woodard. It had been almost a year since Mama died, but the pictures reminded me of her more youthful days. The picture of her in her tennis outfit with a racket in her hand reminded me that she was athletic. She often mentioned bowling and playing softball but did not elaborate, and now I wished she could tell me more.

She made one thing very clear, though: She was terrified of the water. One story she told painted a vivid picture that I would never forget. She said she was standing on the edge of the pool, trying to gain the courage to get in. Suddenly, a boy ran by and pushed her in.

"I was petrified," she said. "I thought I was going to die. People were pointing and laughing, and I was drowning. Finally, someone came over to help me. I was crying so hard I could hardly catch my breath. When I finally got out of the pool, I was furious. I saw that fool who pushed me in. He saw me coming toward him and took off running. I ran after him, around and around that pool. I finally caught him, and when I did, I tried to beat his brains out."

Mama always had a panicked look on her face when she told that story. Recently, I'd seen that same look when she thought her oxygen tank wasn't providing enough air. After I got things under control and calmed her down, she said, "You just don't understand how it feels when you think it's your last breath."

Some of her pictures made me think of Diana Ross and the Supremes. Mama was a beautiful woman with a voice to match. She grew up in Detroit during the height of the Motown era, and many things about her were a reflection of that time. The clothes she wore were exciting, with a dramatic flair. They were colorful and sparkly, and Mama's pictures represented them all. Wigs were also popular in those days. Big hair, long, curly, short, frosted—Mama tried them all.

The picture of her with the big Afro really sparked a memory. Mama loved to dance and always showed us some of the dances she used to do.

We were in the living room, and Mama was playing some albums on the stereo. Dominique and I were lying on the couch. When Mama heard one of her favorite songs, "Dancing in the Street," she started dancing and said, "Yes! That's my song. Come on, Karah—let me show you how it's done." She pushed the coffee table out of the way, and I joined her. "Okay, this is the funky chicken. Stand with your feet apart, like this. Now move your knees in and out. Yes, that's right. Now put your hands like this"—she made a fist with each hand and put them in front of each breast—"and move your elbows up and down. OK, now do it all together. Girl, loosen up; you are too stiff."

Dominique said, "Let me show you," as she bounced up and took over the floor. She started dancing just like Mama but faster. Faster and faster she did it, laughing the entire time.

"Show off," I said.

"You just mad because you can't dance like me," she said as she stuck out her tongue.

"Show us another one, Mama," I yelled.

"OK, this is the last one. I got to finish cooking. Now this is an easy one; it's called the Jerk. Now put your hands like this again." She put her fists in front of her breasts again. "This time, take one down and one up over your head, and take your head up at the same time, like this. OK, you try." I tried it. "Now jerk with it. Loosen up, Karah, loosen up. Girl, you are too doggone stiff. Let Dominique show you. I got to go see about my food."

Her pictures also introduced her family. First, there was Stan. He stood or sat with her in several shots. Then Tony appeared. There were no baby pictures of them but several of me—I wondered why. Maybe it was a change in finances or technology. Or maybe it was because I was the first girl. Nevertheless, there I was, usually with someone holding me. There was one with me sticking my finger in my birthday cake. It always made me smile. Finally, there was Dominique cradled in Mama's arms. Missing from the photos, however, were the men in her life over the years. She mentioned a few, but the only man on her wall was our dad, and that spoke volumes for me.

There was a graceful transition, and the most recent pictures presented a total transformation. Mama reached a point when she no longer liked her picture taken, and she made that clear to everyone. We always tried to respect that, but, thankfully, there were times when we insisted. Mama was much thicker by then, and her hair was short and natural, revealing her snow-white widow's peak. While she dressed for comfort in her later days, her style and flair were never lost. She usually wore colorful muumuu dresses. She said they were the easiest for her to put on. Everyone knew how much she liked them, even my old military buddies. People would send them to her often. Soon, she had a variety of them in all styles and colors. In her most recent picture, she sat in her beautiful muumuu, surrounded by family and friends, looking like the queen she was.

One thing, however, never changed over the years. In every picture, she displayed those signature eyebrows, which only she could apply so perfectly.

Photographs were the easiest to identify with, but many other things brought Mama alive in my mind and heart. Throughout the house were ceramic pieces that she'd painted—cats, both large and small; birds; angels; and a variety of other pieces. Her curio cabinet held her favorites—the black girl and boy, smiling brightly, holding a colorful quilted banner that read "Family"; a full sculpture of Jesus holding a baby in his arms; and a little girl sitting on an alphabet block with the letter A, next to a boy on the one with the Z. She always completed her work by adding "Maxine" or her initials, "MW," on the bottom and the year it was done.

My heart ached, my breath felt short, and tears flowed down my face. No matter how long I stared or how deep my memory, Mama never would sit at the table and paint her ceramics again. I broke down as if she'd just died today. "I know you're resting in the arms of Jesus, Mama," I said. "Rest in peace."

Memories of Mama flooded my mind as I walked from room to room. She was truly an amazing woman. Mama had many talents and skills, and I wanted to be just like her. Cooking was her passion, and she loved being in the kitchen. Mama could cook anything, especially Southern food. She prepared a basic meal of meat, vegetables, and cornbread or biscuits each day. Her collard greens, black-eyed peas, or pinto beans were usually cooked with ham hocks and always seasoned to perfection. Cornbread dressing or macaroni and cheese was typical for Sunday dinner, but Sunday menus were unlimited. Fried chicken, meatloaf, neck bones, or pot roast were common.

During the cooler months, she'd prepare deer sausage, souse meat, or chitterlings. She enjoyed cooking these rare treats, but they were not for us kids. Normally, she called her friends and family members who she knew would enjoy them the most. For us kids, however, her desserts were our favorites. Mama made cakes and pies from scratch. We would all gather around, waiting for our chance to lick the beater or the spoon. She made all sorts of cookies, and the smell would summon the neighborhood. They became so popular that she sold them for a while. Her famous peanut butter cookies kept people stopping by, asking if she still sold them long after she'd stopped.

Banana pudding made from scratch usually was time-consuming, but Mama made it quickly and taught me her valuable shortcut. Mama also made ice cream, and we had a malt machine in which ice cream was turned into our favorite milkshakes. I lost my desire for those, however, when I saw her adding castor oil to my shake when I was sick.

Occasionally, she would make candy, usually for candied or caramel apples. Her favorite candy was peanut brittle, and when she made it, she wasn't as quick to share. Mama also made her own alcoholic beverages. She made wine from seasonal fruit or berries and homebrew (beer). She was so proud of her beer that she bought a label maker and bottle topper to preserve and display her product.

Mama could always make something out of nothing. She made floral arrangements, potholders, and dishtowels that matched her holiday theme. She often made clothes for me and my sister. It was common to see patterns cut out and pinned to material for our new outfits. After she'd sewn them, she'd call us in to try them on.

I could visualize her standing there in one of her many housecoats. Most of them buttoned down the front and had two big pockets on each side. The pockets usually held a tape measure or small scissors. "Be still, girl," she'd mutter, with the stick-pins perched between her lips. She often made matching outfits for me and Dominique when we were growing up. *What were the last ones she made for us?* I asked myself. I couldn't remember. Nevertheless, when she made Dominique's wedding dress, everyone was amazed.

Over the years, Mama had more than her share of pain. She'd lost her mama, daddy, and all four of her sisters. Our dad was only twenty-six when he died in a boating accident. I could only imagine Mama's devastation during that time, as a young widow with four children—Stan was six, Tony was four, I was two years old, and Dominique was only two months.

From my earliest recollection, Victor was the man in our lives, and he was vicious. He added the only negativity to my fun memories of Mama in the kitchen—he once threw a pot of green beans and potatoes clear across the room as he screamed, "I don't want no damn green beans!" That, however, was not the worst episode. They were always arguing and fighting, usually about money and women. Apparently, Victor had too many women and not enough money. One fight happened while we were at school. When my class came out for recess, I could see the police and an ambulance at my house. I started running home, but the teacher caught up to me and grabbed my arm.

"Karah, no, no; I cannot let you go," she said. "Someone will come to get you."

Nobody came. Once school was out, I ran home as fast as I could. When I got there, only Stan was there, sitting at the table. "Come here, Karah," he said. "They been fighting again, and Mama had to go to the hospital. They took Victor to jail." Stan banged his fist on the table, and I started crying. "Come on, Karah. Mama is going to be all right. We will be all right."

A few days later, Mama's sisters came from Detroit and took control of the house. One of them brought her two sons. Mama was the baby sister and was about the same age as these two nephews. She told us they were best friends and had had many adventures together, especially in their teenage years. They cooked and cleaned and made sure we had what we needed, and they never stopped talking about how they were going to get Victor for what he did.

When Mama came home from the hospital, she went straight to her room. Everybody kept telling us to keep the noise down. When Mama finally came out to go to the bathroom, my heart ached. She looked broken. She walked very slowly and wore dark sunglasses. I asked why she had on sunglasses in the house, and my aunt said the light gave her a headache. Mama didn't say anything, but she tried to give us a hug. I felt her hands tremble when she tried to hug me, and she let out a painful groan.

"Okay, Maxie, let's get you back to bed," my aunt said as she held on to Mama.

Victor never came back the entire time they were there, but as soon as they left, he was back, creating problems. It was awful. Every day he and Mama would argue and fight. Cousins, neighbors, friends— everybody came to her rescue, but Victor made it clear it was not their business.

One day Victor was whipping Stan, but Stan would not cry. He hit him over and over; Stan still would not cry. Finally, Mama got between them and screamed, "I said don't hit him no more!" That was the beginning of the end for Victor.

Soon afterward, Mama filed for divorce, and Victor was out of our lives. Unfortunately, he had damaged us all to the core. Sadly, for as long as I can remember, she never had a man to help her or love her; they only added to her pain.

I have tried not to allow her bad relationships to harden my heart, but I learned, from watching her struggle and fight, never to be dependent on any man. It still angered me to think a man would try to hurt my mama, but I was just a little girl. *If only we had been older*, I often thought. Yet I always told myself that God knows best.

When I got pregnant at sixteen, I knew Mama was disappointed. She kept emphasizing that I was going to raise my own child. When Tynisha was born, however, I saw that it warmed her heart. Then I had Dewayne and then Kimberly. Mama did what she could to help me, but I was a proud, responsible mother and did everything I could as a young parent. I was never concerned with hanging out with friends or going out. I just took care of my children and went back to school. We were doing OK, but I knew our future was limited. I decided to join the army, but I needed Mama to take care of the kids until I completed basic training.

Immediately, she said no, that her nerves were too bad. A few days later, though, she changed her mind. She kept them through my basic training, and when I was stationed in Germany, she felt it was best for them to stay with her. When I was assigned to Hawaii, I asked Mama to come with me, and she did. She loved being in Hawaii, and my military family loved her. She still loved to cook and soon everyone valued her skills in the kitchen, as well as her other talents. She became as valuable and respected in the military community as she was back home.

About a year later, unfortunately, Tony was in a car/train collision, and he did not survive. Nothing was ever the same after that. Tony was Mama's baby boy, and he adored his mother. Their relationship was special. He had open-heart surgery when he was about sixteen, after which he had to depend on Mama a lot. He never forgot the sacrifices she made for him. He did everything he could for her and always made her feel his love and appreciation. His death, in addition to the other struggles she'd faced, created a web from which she could not free herself.

After Tony's death, Mama fell into a deep depression, and she later had a stroke. For the next few years, she suffered one health crisis after another. She was in and out of the hospital. She was a fighter, though, and her doctors always seemed amazed by her recovery. She got strong again and came to Georgia to be with the kids while I went to the Persian Gulf. In her later years, COPD was her primary ailment. She had an oxygen machine but always complained of not having enough air. Usually things could be resolved at home, but sometimes she had to go to the hospital.

For her eightieth birthday, we had a big party. She was so happy to see her family and friends all gathered in her honor. I have never forgotten the look on her face when we released a bunch of light-purple balloons. She watched intently as they flew up towards the heavens. She just kept watching them, and I got a strange feeling about the way she kept watching them fly higher and higher. During that time of her life, she always complained about being tired. "I'm just tired," she'd say. "I'm just so tired." Maybe as she watched those balloons, she was telling God she was tired and that she wanted to come home. A few months later, everyone was devastated when her occasional trip to the hospital ended with her lying in a coma for days.

Over the years, Mama and I often talked about what we each of us wanted when one outlived the other. Mama and I had a strong relationship. Ever since she agreed to take care of the kids when I went into the army, she became my dependent. I was a single parent, but the military identified her as the primary care provider, should I be deployed or something worse. She was provided with health care and access to all shopping facilities. That status continued after I married, as my husband was also a soldier. She helped raise all my children and grandchildren. If she didn't come where I was stationed at the time, they went home to her. (They all loved their granny and had some colorful stories to tell.) When it came to her health, she trusted me to be strong enough to make the best decisions. We used to talk about our kids and make light of the situation.

"Don't you go and leave me here with your buck-wild children," she'd say.

"No, don't you leave me here," I'd reply. "You know they are going to be crying a river, and I can't take it."

We laughed about those possibilities so many times, but we were both strong in our faith, and we trusted and believed that God makes no mistakes, and no matter what, all is well. She also made it clear to all the others who loved her: "Don't leave me hooked to those machines." But God knows it takes strength of indescribable proportions to agree to unplug the machines that are sustaining life to the one you love so dearly. Ultimately, the decision was made, and still, to everyone's amazement, Mama lived for almost twelve hours after they unplugged her. She had to leave one final reminder: Death is in God's time, not ours.

The entire family struggled to find peace and comfort since her death. Dominique was in and out of the hospital with ailment after ailment. Stan spoke of watching Mama's favorite television shows, as though he could feel a connection to her through them. "Guess I'll go watch *Walker*. Mama know she loved some *Walker Texas Ranger*," he said. These two were my brother and sister, and there was nothing I could do to take away their pain.

And my poor child Tynisha went into the house, talking to Mama as if she was still in there. ("Now, Granny, you know I want some of your good food, and I can't smell a thing cooking.") Kimberly, on the other hand, couldn't even go in the house. She had taken care of Mama's financial business, so they talked most often. Dewayne didn't say much, but his constantly putting Mama's pictures on Facebook spoke volumes.

My youngest son was born 10 years after Kimberly and affectionately referred to all as Baby-boy. As the baby and especially after the loss of his father, he was special to us all. Nevertheless, he was the apple of mama's eye and she made that very clear. You couldn't say a bad thing about Baby-boy; he could do no wrong in her eyes. I would tell her, "I'm going to put him out," and she'd say, "And he can come right over here with me." Or he'd call her to say I was doing this or that to him. Then she'd sincerely insist that I leave him alone. Baby-boy moved into her house after the funeral and refused to change a thing.

Each of her great-grandchildren also had their own unique relationships with their granny. I couldn't begin to imagine their pain. Just the mention of her name made their eyes water. Everyone was trying to be strong for the other, yet I was sure that, as with me, there were many days they just wanted to call Granny.

Everyone who knew her had a story to tell. She was one of the longest-living family members and oldest members of the neighborhood. Everyone had their favorite memories to treasure, and those will live on forever. I was sure that there were times when they just wanted to call her for something. Maybe they wanted to hear one of her jokes or tell her one. Maybe they needed instructions on cooking something. Or maybe they broke something and couldn't figure out how to fix it. Their pants need hemming, their plants were dying, they had sore throats—whatever they needed, Granny would have the answer, but now they couldn't call her.

So while my heart ached, I knew I was not alone. We touched her heart as she touched ours. Then God said, "It is done." Rest in peace, Granny, and God will give us peace as well.

2

New York City State of Mind

The events of Mama's death had a lasting effect on me. So many emotions seemed to exacerbate my lingering health problems. I felt sick all the time. My stomach felt nauseated, my body ached, my headaches became more frequent, and my blood pressure was elevated. I just did not feel well. I wanted to lie down all the time. Some mornings I was so exhausted and stiff I could barely get out of bed. I didn't sleep well, and I had panic attacks. Several times my heart raced so fast I thought I was having a heart attack and ended up in the emergency room. Time after time, I was given more medication, which ultimately created more issues, especially on my job.

I worked as a supervisor in hospital nutrition. My job requirements were not overwhelming. In fact, I had done well and maintained my position for over seven years. I supervised twenty-five employees, and I enjoyed training and managing them until my health increasingly became an issue. Every day I struggled to get dressed and get to work on time. I had meetings to attend, deadlines to meet, and schedules to make, on top of managing employee issues. It became overwhelming. I lost my patience several times, and my supervisors questioned my outburst. Every day I had a pounding headache. Several times I went to employee health, where they found my blood pressure was extremely high. I was sent to the emergency room, where they administered medication to get it down. When they couldn't get it down, I had to be hospitalized. Eventually, I just couldn't do it anymore. I loved my job, and I was well respected by my peers and my subordinates, but it was just too much. I became increasingly frustrated and prayed to God for guidance. Suddenly, I had a new revelation. Most of the medication was increased as I was trying to maintain my current lifestyle. It was time to downsize. I had to reduce every stressful thing in my life.

One morning after I got to work, I was so tired and in so much pain I went straight to my supervisor's office. "How much notice is required before I resign my position?" I asked.

Her eyes widened as she looked at me in disbelief. "One month is required for supervisors," she replied. "Why? What's going on?"

"I want to make it effective today," I replied. Even I was startled by the words, but my mouth would not stop moving. She tried to suggest some alternatives, but it was clear to me that this was the time, so I turned in my notice.

I told my employees about my decision, and they were heartbroken. We had worked so well together, and they did not want to see me go, but the decision was final. I worked out my notice and said my goodbyes.

On my last day, they had a beautiful going-away party for me. People came from all over the hospital to express their well wishes. It was heartwarming to hear so many people acknowledge and express their appreciation for the contributions I'd made while employed there. Yet as I walked to my car with my arms filled with flowers and balloons, my heart felt empty. The days and weeks to follow felt even emptier and devoid of substance. My mind wandered as I examined my new existence—kids all grown, Mama gone, no mate, no job, no purpose. I was just … there.

When Naomi, my best friend, called, it was like a spark of magic for me. She had a way of lifting my spirits no matter what was going on. "Karah, guess what?" she said in a slow, playful way.

"What have you done, girlie?" I asked cheerfully. "Are you pregnant?"

"What? Heck no! Not even close." She laughed uproariously.

"Well, are you getting married again?"

"Absolutely not."

"OK, what, girlie, what? What has you so excited?"

"Effective May first, yours truly is being promoted to lieutenant colonel."

"Oh my God, oh my God!" I screamed. "Girlie, that is the best news I've heard in a long time."

"Yes, they finally realized who is running things around here," she said, and I could almost see the smirk on her face. "Karah, I really, really, really—I mean, *really*—want you to come. Say yes, please."

"Of course I'll be there. I am so excited."

"We are going to have a ball. I can't wait to see you."

"Me too. This is perfect timing for me."

"I'll make my flight arrangements in the morning."

"Oh, girlie, try to fly into FFBP—that's the private airport that the military uses primarily for official business flights, and it's much cheaper," she explained. "Call me with the details so I can pick you up."

Later, I made the arrangements and called Naomi with the arrival time.

For the next few weeks, I got prepared. I was ready to see the big city.

Then Naomi called at the last minute, explaining that her commander had set a mandatory meeting, and neither she nor her daughter, Shelly, could pick me up from the airport. She gave me every detail of her well-thought-out plans for me. I listened and took extensive notes, but panic immediately set in. Prior to that moment, I hadn't even known her address.

I never expressed any concerns to her. I was honored when she told me she was getting promoted and needed my assistance with her ceremony. She would never know, but those plans made me a nervous wreck. I was accustomed to being in control, and trust was a major issue for me. Taking a taxi from a remote airport through New Jersey with no clue as to where I was going created a problem in my mind. I would have preferred getting a rental car and using my GPS to find her house. But she had already made it clear that getting a rental from and back to that location would be inconvenient. She owned two vehicles and needed me to drive one, so I could get family members on and off the base.

When the pilot announced that we would be landing in fifteen minutes, my mind flipped into strictly business mode. We landed on the tarmac and walked up some steps into the terminal. The place was small and empty. I walked with a straight face and tried to look unassuming as I followed the signs to baggage claim. I couldn't help but notice there were no taxis lined up in front, as with larger airports. I got my bags and headed for the only attendant I saw.

"May I help you?" he asked in a thick African accent.

"Yes, where can I get a taxi?"

"Are you military?" he asked.

"Yes," I replied.

"Can I see some identification, please?"

I put down my bags, scrambled through my purse until I found my ID, and then handed it to him.

"OK, Sergeant Woodard," he said after a brief look. "Use this phone"—he handed me one he was holding—"and press *talk*. Someone will assist you."

The person on the other end of the phone told me to keep holding the phone, and someone would contact me shortly. About ten minutes later, the phone rang, and I was asked to raise my hand. I did as I was directed, and the taxi driver walked over to me. He greeted me with a big smile and introduced himself.

"Let me help you with your bags," he said.

After taking the phone back to the attendant, we headed out to the taxi. He asked where I was going, and when I gave him the address, he said we'd be there in about thirty minutes. I was so relieved. *At least there's a way to track me if I go missing*, I thought. When we reached his van, there were already two soldiers in uniform waiting inside. It was just like old times. I'd often traveled in vans or small buses throughout my military career. As a soldier, no matter the mode of transportation or how long the trip, I was most comfortable among other soldiers.

We immediately introduced ourselves. Along the way we talked nonstop about the military. They were each going to the base for a temporary duty assignment. I was surprised to learn that Fort Dix, where I had attended basic training and advanced training, was now a part of this base, now called McGuire-Dix-Lakehurst. It was not likely that they would meet Naomi, but I still mentioned her, just in case they crossed paths. My stop was first so I didn't get to see the base.

"Nice meeting you both," I said.

"Thank you for your service, ma'am," one of them said as I exited.

"And thank you for yours. Enjoy your careers," I replied.

"Let me help with your bags," the driver said.

"No, I'm good; thank you very much."

As I walked up the long driveway, my phone rang; it was Naomi.

"Hey, girlie, where are you?"

"Just got to the house," I replied.

"Okay, Shelly is on her way, but Mom is inside. I'll be there as soon as this meeting is over."

No sooner had we hung up than the door opened, and there stood Mrs. Lahaina. We gave each other a nice hug.

"Mama, how are you?"

"I'm okay, Karah. How was your flight?"

"It was nice and smooth."

"Come in; you're at home, you know."

"Yes, ma'am."

In walked two hound dogs, wagging their tails and smiling as if they knew I was like family.

"Can I get you something to drink, Karah?"

"No, ma'am, I'll get it; you just relax."

"That's all I do, Karah. Relax, relax—that's all I do."

"Auntie!" an energetic voice yelled as the door was flung open.

"Shelly," I said, "look at you, girl. You are beautiful."

"Oh, thank you, Auntie. You are too kind." She gave me the biggest hug. "I'm so glad you're here. Mom misses you."

"I miss her too. I can't wait to see her."

"Come on, Auntie, let me show you where your room is. This place is going to get crowded very soon."

I followed as Shelly bounced up the stairs. "Hope it's just the trip that has me tired because if not, I will have to limit my trips up and down these steps throughout the day. Whew!" I exclaimed as I got to the top. "Girl, those steps are rough."

"You'll get use to it, Auntie. In a couple of days, you'll be running up and down like me."

"Yeah, right," I said, and we both laughed.

"Hey, sunshine, where are you?" a voice called from downstairs. "Come on down here, sunshine."

Like a little kid, I jumped up and ran down the stairs. Screaming each other's names out loud, we grabbed each other and held on tightly, gently rocking each other back and forth. The exciting reunion went on and on.

"Come on, girlie, let me show you around. This place is going to get crazy soon."

"That's what Shelly told me when she showed me to my room."

"Oh, girlie, you'll see—my family is on the way. It's going to be a Hawaiian invasion. Let start outside before it gets too dark, just in case you want to take a walk in the morning."

"Sounds good," I replied. "You know I still love the mornings."

"If you go out, let the dogs out too. They love being outside. You don't have to watch them too closely. They won't leave this yard. But bring them back in when you come back. They like to dig when no one's watching."

"No problem, but you know I'm not picking up poop or wiping the dogs' butts. I thought it was a joke when you first told me that."

"No joke. These dogs know, so as soon as I bring them back inside, they just stand there looking up at the baby wipes and waiting their turn."

I laughed at that description. "Girl, you are too funny. I'm so glad I came. Your personality is infectious, and I need to catch some of that."

"Karah, I love it here. It's so quiet, and when I leave Uncle Sam, I don't want to think about him until I go back to work. There are plenty places for me to relax around here. Now, this front porch—I love to sit here and watch the traffic. I can see the cars, but they can't see me. There's a deck on the back," she said as we walked around the house."

"Wow, this is huge," I said as I looked out over the property.

"Yes, I need my space."

We walked amid oak trees as she showed me the borders to the property. Once back at the house, she took me onto the back deck and pointed out the stationary bike and treadmill. "It's all yours. Feel free to use this stuff any time. I want you to feel at home here. Tomorrow is my big day."

"Yes, congratulations again. I can't hardly fathom that you're a senior officer."

"Girl, when they told me, I had to pinch myself. Seems like just yesterday I was a PFC in that little-ass kitchen at West Point."

"Oh, my God, girl—wasn't that a mess?"

"Yes, but we handled it, didn't we."

"Yes, we did—you, me, and Lori; three meals a freaking day. That girl was a hard worker too. I often wonder where she is."

"Yeah, me too. I tried to find her on the internet a few times but couldn't."

"She probably married that guy, Wayne. You know, Wayne the pain in my ..."

We laughed hysterically. Later that evening, Naomi and Shelly came to my room where we continued to talk for hours, trying to catch up.

The next morning I was awakened by voices downstairs. I'd overslept. I jumped up, got dressed, and went downstairs. It was not an exaggeration; there truly was a Hawaiian invasion. People were all over the house, which a few hours earlier had seemed too huge to fill. Naomi's family had arrived—adults, kids, some eating, some reading, most just lounging. Some I knew from previous visits to Hawaii. Greetings came from all directions in Hawaiian dialect and broken English.

"Good morning, Auntie. My name is Enu, and this is my twin brother, Eli. We are both in the military too."

"Yes, I heard. Naomi has been bragging on you both. I remember meeting you when I last visited Hawaii. You must have been about six or seven."

"Auntie, much has changed," Eli replied, imitating a deep masculine voice.

"I can see that. Fifteen years bring about lots of growth and development," I said as I looked down at my body.

"Oh, Auntie, you look great. I also heard you were once a drill sergeant, and I know what physical conditioning that requires."

"Oh, speaking of fitness, where is Kay?" I asked.

We all burst into laughter, acknowledging that we all knew Kay was a fitness guru.

"Auntie … you know Mom. She's on that bike or treadmill."

"Dad and Jason took the dogs out."

"Jason?"

"Yes, Auntie, our baby brother."

"Oh my, I forgot about the baby."

"Auntie, that baby is twelve and as tall as we are."

About that time, Kay and the rest of the family came in. Before we could greet each other, Naomi started yelling my name.

"Karah, come here! Hey, everyone, this is my best friend, Karah. Please introduce yourselves."

"Aloha, Karah. I'm Reva, and this is my husband, Thomas; sons, Kyle and Nathan; and baby girl, Sylvia."

"Hi, nice to meet you all," I replied.

"Aloha," Kay said, holding back laughter. "My name is Kay. This is my hubby, Jake; son Jason; and I think you've already met the twins."

"Of course, how have you been Kay?"

"Good to see you; it's been a while."

"And how are you Jake?" I asked.

"I'm good, Karah, and happy to be off the island."

"That I can't even imagine," I replied.

"Just for a visit, Karah, just for a visit."

"I know that's right. I can't wait to visit the island again. Jason, nice to meet you. You are very handsome, just like your brothers."

"Thank you, Auntie; nice to meet you also."

Introductions went on throughout the day as a constant flow of relatives arrived. Many of them lived on the mainland, some near and some as far away as Washington State. They all welcomed me as a member of the family. I did my best to remember names and faces; fortunately, we had a few days together. I wasn't good with names, and many of these were Hawaiian names. *This is going to be a challenge,* I thought.

"Okay, Karah, ride with me," Naomi said. "We need to go to base to make sure things are coming together." Then she yelled to those assembled. "Hey, don't lose track of time. The ceremony is at three. Let's meet back here by noon."

I grabbed a bagel and gave Mama a kiss before we headed out. When we got to Naomi's office, hearing everyone call her *ma'am* was an eye-opening revelation. This girl had done it, and her dad would be so proud. He had been a military man, and when I first met him he spoke so proudly of her. We were just sergeants then, and unfortunately, he'd recently passed away, but I was sure Naomi could feel his spirit from above.

"Ma'am, where do you want these flowers?"

"Just put them here for now."

"Ma'am, what time is the food coming?"

"It should be here before the ceremony starts. If the caterers are not here by 1400 hours, get them on the phone. I don't want any problems. Do you remember the set-up?"

"Yes, ma'am."

"I think so."

"Just follow the diagram," Naomi said. "Karah, please go with them to set up the equipment—utensils, meat, meat, meat, starch, veggies, salad. Got it?"

"Yes, ma'am!" I said with a smirk.

"Oh, I forgot to whom I was speaking; pardon me."

We just laughed. Food service was my field of expertise, and Naomi knew my skills better than anyone.

Once we were back at the house, I immediately went out and sat on the deck. It was heavenly. I just wanted to stay there and get my "Zen" on, but time was passing fast. We all got dressed, and everyone gathered downstairs. "Okay, guys, you all look so beautiful. I will lead the way. Karah, you get behind me since you've never driven to the base. Plus, you need to bring Reva, Thomas, and these boxes. Shelly, you take Mom and the kids. The rest will cram in with one of the twins. Make sure you have your ID cards, or you will be held up at the gate."

There were five vehicles of Hawaiians and me. Things went as planned.

The ceremony began.

"Please stand for the presentation of colors and remain standing through the playing of the national anthem."

Immediately, I thought about my days as a drill sergeant. After every training cycle, I stood before the senior leaders, the families of the trainees, and other guests. It was always a proud moment, and this felt no different. After the prayer, before the official orders were read, Naomi's commander provided some highlights of Naomi's career. Her résumé was long and impressive. She had been stationed in Japan and the Philippines and had worked as a flight nurse before becoming the commander of a health clinic. I marveled as I listened to accolade after accolade. Then came the attention to orders: "The president of the United States, acting upon the recommendation of the secretary of the US Air Force, has placed trust and confidence in the patriotism, integrity, and abilities of Major Naomi Lahaina-Brooks. In view of these special qualities and demonstrated potential to serve in the higher grade, Major Naomi Lahaina-Brooks has demonstrated her ability to fulfill the requirements and is hereby promoted to the permanent rank of lieutenant colonel (LTC), United States Air Force. October 1, 2013"

Shelly went up and pinned the new rank on her mom's uniform. She looked remarkably like her mom when she was that age. They were both beautiful. Cameras flashed throughout the room as we all tried to capture this moment. Shelly stepped to the side of her mother and stood there as she took the oath of office for her new position.

"I, Naomi Lahaina-Brooks," having been appointed a lieutenant colonel in the United States Air Force, do solemnly swear that I will support and defend the Constitution of the United States, against all enemies, foreign and domestic; that I will bear true faith and allegiance to the same; that I take this obligation freely, without any mental reservation or purpose of evasion; and that I will well and faithfully discharge the duties of the office upon which I am about to enter. So help me God."

It was official; my friend Naomi was a lieutenant colonel. As Shelly gave her mom a hug and kiss, Mrs. Lahaina moved slowly toward them. Her mom removed a lei from her neck and loudly stated, "Everyone must get 'lei'd' sometimes." The room erupted in laughter. I heard one of the twins say, "Grandma," as he placed his hands over his face. She placed the lei on her daughter and carefully moved back to her seat.

Everyone clapped as Naomi walked up to the podium to address the audience. She represented the air force well as she stood in her dress-blue uniform adorned with medals and ribbons. It was clear to me that our days in the army together had been just a stepping stone. This was where she belonged.

"Aloha, and thank you all for being here to celebrate with me on this special day. I will be brief," she began cheerfully with a big smile. "Commanders, first sergeants, peers, and subordinates: Aim high! Fly, fight, win! To my family: *Aloha mai no aloha aku o kaa huhu kaa mea e ola ole ai. mahalo*. Translation, for those of you who have forgotten how to speak Hawaiian— 'When love is given, love naturally flows back in return. Thank you all.'" Then she asked me to stand. Shocked at the request, immediately I stood at attention. "This is Sergeant First Class (Retired) Karah Woodard. We have been friends since 1986, almost thirty years. We served together at Fort Campbell, Kentucky, and in Hawaii. She was everything I wished to be as a soldier. She was always professional, always disciplined, gracious, and loyal. And even though she had a family and was a single parent, she was always there for me. She helped me when I was struggling through nursing school, and because of her kindness, I was able to keep my focus and graduate with honors. For that, I am forever grateful. Thank you, Karah. You were always my friend, but from now on, you are my sister."

The twins appeared, one on each side of me. Each placed a white lei around my neck and gave me a kiss on each cheek. "Welcome to the family, Auntie."

"Thank you. It is truly an honor."

Everyone applauded.

"Now let's have some fun!" Naomi yelled. "I have a special treat for you. My sister Reva will perform the hula, our traditional Hawaiian dance. Afterward, please join us in the dining area for traditional island food."

The lights were dimmed as beautiful Hawaiian music started to play. Slowly, Reva entered the quiet room. She had been transformed in to a Hawaiian goddess. Light and dark blue baby's breath filled the leis around her head and on each ankle. She wore two white leis loosely around her neck. Her dark-blue grass skirt sparkled in the dim light.

"I will now dance the Hawaiian dance of friendship," she said. Softly and gracefully, she entertained the crowd. She glided and shimmied from every position, seemingly calling and pulling her audience to her, and then offering them up to the sky. No one moved or said a word. We just watched as we became a part of the theme of this enchanting, hypnotic dance. Up to the heavens, out to the crowd, back and forth, she wheeled us, giving us to the heavens and the heavens to us. Down on one knee, she offered us up, like a plea.

We were all mesmerized, but for me, her message was clear, and I just had to smile. The performance ended to a long and thunderous applause. A crowd of us migrated toward Reva. She happily explained the concepts and tradition of the dance. Most were satisfied, said thank you, and moved to the dining room. Some of us needed just a little more. Enthusiastically, she led us through the steps. After trying a few times, hula dancers gained my respect. While I had learned to dance well over the years, I had to leave this one for the professionals.

The Hawaiian theme continued as we entered the reception area. Light and dark blues created an evening sky, while crystal, glass, and shiny serving equipment sparkled like the stars. Tables overflowed with tropical flowers, fruit, and nuts. Several tables were filled with buttery rolls and pastry that glistened under the heat lamps. Centered in the rear of the room was a huge cake with mounds of white icing. Blue letters spelled out CONGRATULATIONS, MA'AM! One final emphasis was the beautiful fountain, flowing with a blue cocktail. It already had a line of guests. Clearly every effort was given toward making this a realistic Hawaiian experience.

The menu included grilled mahi-mahi, Kalua pig, and Huli-Huli chicken. There was also sticky rice, taro root "mashed potatoes," long-rice noodles, and Hawaiian mixed vegetables. Mac salad and poi was also available. The food brought back so many memories. I'd tried many foods while stationed in Hawaii for four years. After I left the island, I still craved most of the things I'd eaten. Even though I was a well-trained cook, I could not even begin to replicate the recipes.

Our enchanting evening was coming to an end, but as soon as that announcement was made, I hurried to the mic and commanded the room's attention. "This has been an evening to remember, and I'd be remiss if I didn't say a word or two. I have met many amazing people here tonight, and I thank you for your kindness. To Naomi's family— Mrs. Lahaina, your family is truly the best. Thank you for welcoming me. Family love forever. And to you, my precious friend—we started this journey many years ago and had no clue where it would end. Look at us now. I'm retired, and you are still carrying the torch. Be proud, my friend; you deserve this honor. We are all here for you. Everyone, please raise your glasses in one final toast to Lieutenant Colonel Lahaina-Brooks."

The night ended with cheers echoing across the room. Once home, everyone retreated to their spaces to get some sleep. The next morning, we would head to Naomi's next adventure—the Five Boro Bike Tour.

Morning came quickly, and I was so excited. I longed to see New York City. Throughout my military career, I'd visited big cities, and they always energized me. It had been a long time since I'd had that experience, and I was eager to end the drought. My bags were packed, and I had on my walking gear. I had wanted to ride on the bike tour but had missed the deadline to register. So my plan was to enjoy Manhattan, where we would be staying. Downstairs, the house was like a workplace, and everyone was busy. People were going quickly up and down the stairs and in and out of the kitchen continuously as they filled their backpacks with items for the ride.

Mama would not be making the trip—she had expressed her desire to go but ultimately decided it would be too much for her. "Karah, enjoy yourself. The hounds and I will stay here and guard the house *this time*."

Outside the packing continued. Several of the men were loading the bicycles into the back of the pickup truck. Finally, everything was packed, and we were on our way. I rode with Naomi and the bikes.

There wasn't much to see during most of the drive, but the steady flow of traffic allowed my imagination to flow freely. Cars, trucks, motorcycles, and buses were all headed toward the city. I could see signs of their coming adventure in some of them. Many trucks and cars had bicycles attached to them. They were probably going to the big bike ride too. Some vehicles were pulling boats. I was captured by the possibility of their adventures and tried to figure out where the rivers and lakes were in the area. Then, suddenly, there it was—the Big Apple. Once we entered the city, Naomi tried to use her navigation system as I looked out the windows for the Marriott-Marquis. The buildings were so tightly connected that I could hardly read the signs before we had passed them. Car horns honked, people tried to cross the small streets, and big buses drove as if they were sport cars. I was totally consumed by it all.

"It should be on our right, Karah. I don't want to pass it. Oh, look—there it is. But where the heck is the parking?" Slowly passing the building, she turned at the next light and circled the block. "There has to be a side street in here somewhere. Here it is." She pulled up behind a line of cars.

"Yes, girlie, you did it. We are here—New York City," I said.

Shortly thereafter, other family members arrived, and we tried to figure out where to put the bicycles overnight. Naomi and Shelly had very expensive bikes and refused to let them out of their sight. Several suggestions were made.

"Leave them on the back of the truck. They're tied down; no one can steal them," Eli said.

"Oh really? This is New York City, braddah," Enu responded.

"Well, it's too late to take them to the holding area. Who thought of this brilliant idea?" asked Thomas as he looked directly at Naomi.

"Oh no, you don't try to blame Mom," Shelly scolded.

"Well, I'm just asking" Thomas retorted.

"Well, maybe you should have gotten more involved with the planning," Shelly said.

Then Naomi chimed in. "Let's just take them inside."

"And do what with them?" Kay asked.

"We can leave them outside our rooms," Naomi replied.

"These people are not going to let us take bicycles into this hotel," I said.

"Watch," Naomi said.

I stood below and watched as Naomi and the twins took the first three bicycles up. I kept waiting for the hotel attendant or manager to show up, but they made it with no problems. Then it was my turn, I had Jason's bike and struggled to get it into the elevator. People were giving me the evil eye. I acted just like I didn't notice their uppity gestures as I followed my Hawaiian family.

We spent the evening chatting and relaxing as they prepared for the ride. The next morning, everyone gathered their gear and headed downstairs. Taking the bicycles onto the elevators was more chaotic this time. More people were going down and, surprisingly, more than the Lahaina family seemed to have had this idea. Finally, they were all down and on their way. They waved goodbye and left me standing in the middle of Times Square. The bike riders would soon be coming through this area, and we had identified a few spots for me to stand.

It was a beautiful sunny day but kind of cool, so I went back to the room to get my sunglasses and a sweater. Before I left the room, I looked out the window at this unbelievable city. I noticed something unusual happening with cars on a huge platform. I watched until I figured out what was going on. The platform at ground level filled with cars in two or three rows with eight or ten cars each. Once it was full, it went down into the ground, and the next platform came down to be filled. *Now this is amazing*, I thought. *New York City has given new meaning to the use of elevators.*

I made it to my spot again and watched as thousands of bikes rode through Manhattan. I called out words of encouragement as Naomi and her clan passed me on the sidewalk. They looked like they were having such a good time. This was an annual event, and I told myself I would be ready next time. I was all alone in Times Square, but I wasn't bored for a second. I felt safe; there were cops everywhere. They were on horses, scooters, and bikes, as well as on foot. It hadn't been long since the Boston Marathon bombing, and everyone was on high alert.

Naomi and the others would not return until around five, so I was going sightseeing.

As I looked around, everything was innovative and amazing. Standing in this square was like nothing I could have imagined. Slowly, I marveled at every inch of this spectacular place. There were so many buses, big and small. Some had open tops, but they were all filled with people, and they all had messages on the sides—they were like moving billboards. Some buses advertised department stores; some had ads for sexy jeans, underwear, jewelry, or perfume. They were all alluring. This place was alive. Huge Jumbotrons reached out over the small, overcrowded space, captivating the imaginations of passersby, many of whom had to stop and pull out their devices to capture the futuristic exhibition commanding their attention. The advertisement for the Broadway show *Kinky Boots* mesmerized me. The background was a seductive, vivacious red, and two boots came together in a sexy way to make the K in *Kinky*—genius. It didn't make me want to see the play as much as it made my creative juices flow. I wanted to be sitting around a table with the people who created that marketing strategy, sharing ideas, making it all come together. I wanted to be associated with that league.

Suddenly, a Mercedes M-class seemingly rolled on to the screen. It was huge, and the steel-gray color was so realistic. Again, it didn't make me want to purchase it or even ride in it. No, I wanted to be a part of this presentation. This place was what I needed for inspiration. My greatest desire was to become a writer, a well-respected author, and this place said yes!

I walked over to the crowded bleachers, climbing past many people eating and taking pictures, until I got to the top. There I stood, looking out at the iconic place where the ball dropped on New Year's Eve. I'd seen many places in my lifetime, especially during my military career. Nothing, however, had ever been so captivating for me as Times Square. For hours, inspiration after inspiration captivated and mesmerized me. How could I reach this grand stage? How could one of my books reach this level and be displayed here for all to see?

Maybe one would be made into a Broadway play. My mind wandered through the realms of possibilities.

Suddenly, there on the street was Cookie Monster and two other Sesame Street characters. People surrounded the trio, wanting a picture with the famous characters. I had to have something to show Naomi, so I when down and waited my turn. This feat, however, was not easy. Cookie Monster grabbed me and pulled me close to get the shot, but I missed. My camera phone did not have the front-facing feature so I had to guess if we were in the shot. Looking at the picture, I saw I'd cut off his head.

"One more?" I said. Again, he pulled me close. I took the shot.

"Did you get it?" he asked.

I looked at the camera. "No."

He stomped comically.

I tried again and again with no luck. "This is the last time; I promise," I said. After trying again, I gave him a few dollars as I walked away, looking at the shot, "Damn—missed again." I had to laugh at the situation. Baby-Boy kept telling me to get a real phone.

I walked to the corner and spoke with one of the open-top–bus drivers to find out more about the tour. The price was fair and sounded exciting, so I boarded the bus and climbed to the top. I wanted to see everything. The tour guide talked to us throughout the entire tour, pointing out homes of the stars, monuments and shopping places.

He pointed out the crane that was in recent news. It was still suspended in mid air. Shortly thereafter, he directed us to an area and said, "and this is ground zero".

I felt a chill. We didn't officially take a moment of silence, but the tour guide didn't say another word until we'd passed the area.

The bus tour was a "hop on/hop off" type, but I wasn't feeling too adventurous. I just wanted to stay on the bus and look. When the tour was over, I asked the driver about living in this area.

He told me that he was retired military. "The town takes good care of veterans."

I was excited as I went on my way. I stopped at a pizza stand to have a slice of "Famous New York Pizza," according to the sign. While there, I met the cutest couple. They were from New Zealand and very friendly. We stood there, eating pizza and sharing our admiration for this amazing city.

It was dark when I returned, and Naomi and crew had also returned. We changed and, after much consideration, went to dinner at Bubba Gump's and shared our adventures. The next day we seemed to walk every inch of Time Square. Central Park was beautiful. Horse-drawn carriages lined the roads. Wall Street, Trump Tower, Macy's, Motown, and New York pizza all made it into my collection of pictures. We hit every store, vender, and restroom within that three-mile radius, it seemed, but it was not enough for me.

On our way back to the hotel, we stopped for a few minutes to catch our breath, and I could not help but notice four black girls. They looked like college students, ready for a weekend of "girls gone wild." Their hair and makeup were flawless. Their dresses were short, and one kept tugging on her hem. Their heels were high, and it was obvious that they were not adept at walking in them. Still, they looked like they were having the time of their lives. I overheard them talking about how much fun they were going to have at Jay Z's club. They reminded me of my oldest granddaughter, who was in college and was likely having a similar experience.

"Okay, girlie, let's get these bags to the room," I heard Naomi say.

God bless them, I thought as I smiled and walked away.

We spent the rest of the evening having cocktails and looking out the window, while resting in the arms of this beautiful city. I had big dreams, and this experience lit a fire in me like never before. I was certain that my NYC inspirations would live in my heart forever and hopefully rekindle my greatest ambitions. However, there was one more thing Naomi and I had to do before I left for home.

Life is beautiful, and no matter what, I always see the glass as half full. Naomi is far more optimistic than I am. Her glass is always overflowing, and if not, you would never know. I could always depend on her to lift me up and make me smile when things were gloomy. In one case, however, both of us were robbed of that ability. For different reasons, each of our husbands now lay in Arlington National Cemetery.

We made the three-hour drive to the cemetery with little

conversation. This would be the first time we had gone there together, and neither of us knew what to say. The atmosphere was devoid of humor or small talk. Thoughts flooded my mind, and I was certain Naomi was having the same experience. Our situations were much different. My husband got sick, and I was with him the entire time. He lived for eighteen months after his diagnosis. He died in our living room one afternoon as I was preparing lunch. He had cancer. He never smoked or drank and ran with the fast group during fitness class. He'd gone to the doctor for a crackling sound in his ear, and they found the cancer. How did he get this disease? That was the only mystery I faced regarding his death.

The death of Naomi's husband, however, was a total mystery. He had just retired from the army. He was living in their home in Hawaii. Naomi was on assignment and hadn't seen him in weeks. He was found dead and had been there for several days. Things became more unbelievable when she returned to their home. Strange people were coming to the house, saying things that alarmed her. One man said, "Did you really know who your husband was? I know a man who can tell you everything." He wanted her to meet someone who, he said, would tell unknown things about her husband. She refused.

People also came to their home, insisting on retrieving items they'd left there. Some tried to force their way in to look for things. She had to call the police. I knew the story, and it had her terrified. I did not want to hear her recount it again. Together, we would show respect to our husbands and leave all unanswered questions for a different time and place.

We went inside the Welcome Center at Arlington and obtained a map with the address and location of our loved ones. We drove around the huge cemetery, searching for the location. We found my husband's gravesite first. I knew his resting place overlooked the Pentagon. We stood there for a while, admiring the large marble headstone on which two hearts were entwined.

"That's beautiful, Karah."

"Yes, it is. You know, I will be buried with him someday. My name and information will go right below those words."

"Oh, girlie, I don't even want to think about that. Let's take some pictures."

We took several shots, and then it was time to say goodbye.

"I'll give you two some time alone," Naomi said. "I can hear you telling me to go, George. I'm going, I'm going," she teased as she walked away.

Memories flooded my mind. Our life together had been good. "I have your only child. How? Why did you leave me? Now I'm all alone to raise him. Father, please, I trust in your decision. Please give me peace," I said with tears running down my face. It was heart-wrenching. I had been there many times, but this time was different. My mama was gone. Our son was struggling to find his way in the world. And I felt his father's absence more now than ever before.

Suddenly, Naomi started calling my name repeatedly. I wiped my face and said goodbye to my husband. When I turned, I saw her standing across the cul-de-sac in the middle of rows of crosses.

"I found Allen!" she yelled. "They live across the street from each other!"

You have got to be kidding me, I thought, looking up toward the heavens. I hurried over, and there he lay, less than five hundred feet from my husband.

3

Youthful Thinking

After my trip I simply could not stop thinking about New York City. The energy of that place ignited the fuel that brought all my passions back to life. Deep inside, I always yearned for a change, a different lifestyle. The saying "Shoot for the moon and always be among the stars" resonated in my mind. In other words, set your goals high and accept no limits. Ultimately, you'll find yourself surrounded by others who share that philosophy. While I practiced that principle, somehow I always ended up amid a battle. I often thought maybe I was simply born to be a soldier. Adapting to extreme situations is one of the most important abilities a soldier must demonstrate, and that was the story of my life.

Having an active lifestyle was always important to me. I grew up swimming and playing tennis. I also walked a lot and did various exercises on the floor of my bedroom. When I had my children, physical activities became the preferred option for family outings. It was the most economical, kept the children entertained, and it always tired them out. So when they were younger, we went to different parks. Sometimes we played ball, threw the Frisbee, or flew kites. Most often, however, I sat and watched as they played on the swings and climbed on the equipment. As soon as they were old enough, everyone was taught to swim and roller skate. Skating became everyone's favorite activity. We spent many memorable weekends at the skating rink. Over the years, regardless of their ages, skating remained a part of our activities. Even my grandchildren enjoyed this long-standing tradition. Many birthday celebrations were held at the skating rink, including my own. When we weren't skating, we usually engaged in some other physical activity. I always considered myself as physically fit. When I join the army, however, physical fitness took on a totally different meaning.

During basic training, everything a soldier did was designed to enhance stamina and endurance—not only the standard exercises like running, pushups, and sit-ups but during all phases of training. Going to the rifle range, standing in long lines for chow, taking apart your weapon and putting it back together in fifteen seconds—everything we did was a strategic part of the training. I didn't understand the concept until I became a drill sergeant and a part of the planning process. I guess the same idea can be applied to life in general. Every issue we face will strengthen us, teach us, and make us wiser.

My fitness knowledge was above average, but my fitness condition was far below. I was about thirty pounds over my normal weight. Most people swore they couldn't tell. They'd say I was just thick or that I carried it well. Maybe they were being kind or maybe it was the clothes I wore, but I was fat and out of shape. I was so low on the fitness chart that if I could just get up, get dressed, and get outside every day, I would see that as a success. So that is where I started. I just focused on, *No excuses; get out that door*. For the first few days, however, I struggled. Despite that simple objective, something always came up. One day I overslept, then I had a stomachache, then no clean sweat pants, my eye hurt, my butt itched—there was always something.

Then I finally started to get in the groove. If I didn't have clean workout clothes, it was my own fault. I just put on something and went. If I forgot to charge my music source, it was my fault. I had to exercise for at least an hour without music or wait until it was charged. As I became more consistent, however, other issues arose. I started feeling dizzy during my walks. Many things had to be considered, such as whether to eat something before I walked. If so, what? Should I drink lots of water or sports drinks?

When we did fitness in the military, we just got up and did it, usually on an empty stomach—not even water until we finished. Damn, was I just getting old? There were older soldiers in the military, and they had to do physical training, just like everyone else. I had to figure out what was best for me. Finally, I got a fanny pack, and I put in a bottle of water that just fit the size. My music source and a small towel also fit. I didn't want anything in my hands. I turned it around, so the bottle fit in the center of my back. I put on my headset and ran the cord down my back under my clothes. I could not have any distractions, and this worked perfectly.

There were several areas around town where I liked to walk, but the university campus was my favorite. I had gone to school there, and I knew their fitness center opened early, and there was always someone walking or running out there. It was a large area with many optional routes, none of which took me repeatedly past my car. I didn't need the temptation of getting in and going home too soon. I liked walking out a certain distance and back. I usually walked alone, and this area was very well lit. Several different security agencies also patrolled the area, including the university police, a contracted security agency, and the city police. So when I walked, I felt safe. I walked as often as I could.

I didn't set fitness goals for myself immediately. I just wanted to relieve some stress, stretch my body, and strengthen my core. All I did was walk. Sometimes slow, sometimes a little faster, but I walked. Distance didn't matter either; I let my body dictate how far. Day after day, I got my stuff together and went on my walk. I loved the sun on my face and taking deep breaths of the crisp morning air. I focused on keeping my posture erect and stomach in. I kept my arms up like I was running to the beat of my music. I preferred rap music for my walk because the rhythm was perfect, and the lyrics kept me entertained. It was poetry to my ears—sometimes a little vulgar, but expressing raw emotions may require a few choice words. Plus, I was a grown-up, free to choose, and it wasn't illegal. I knew it would not influence my behavior, and God knew my heart.

I started to notice several ladies on a regular basis. They also noticed me, and we'd smile at each other and wave. One day one of them mouthed something to me. I took off my headset, and she repeated, "I love your energy." That was inspiring to hear. She was right; my music energized me. Although sometimes I just had to laugh and say to myself, *Damn, Weezie, it's too early to be talking about coochie.*

Many days when I got back home and took a hot Epsom salts bath, I went back to bed. This was my regimen, and I did it for months with seemingly no physical change. In fact, someone else must have also noticed. I was just walking along, listening to my headset, when a car pulled over on the opposite side of the narrow street. When the window came down, I saw it was an old friend of mine. He worked on campus and said he just stopped to say hi. We were going in the same direction, so I just turned off my music and talked as he drove along slowly, keeping pace with me.

Soon, though, he started to offer unsolicited advice. He worked in the athletic department and obviously felt he was an expert on my fitness needs. He suggested that I jog a little and maybe change my diet to get the weight off.

"OK," I said, "I'm trying." I thought, *Who asked you?* But I just smiled as he continued to drive along and talk.

"I eat the same breakfast every morning—oatmeal and a banana," he said. "Then for lunch I have a big salad, and for dinner—" A car came up behind him then, so he had to drive away, but as he did, he called out, "I'll come by your house so we can finish talking."

Wow, I thought as I turned my music back on. Lil Wayne was cussing enough for both of us, so I just got lost in his lyrics. Despite that shocking encounter, the place was alive, and I looked forward to getting out there every morning.

My music kept me entertained, but what motivated me even more was the sight of military recruits running in formation. The university had a ROTC program that afforded me that opportunity. Day after day, I'd pass them, or they'd pass me as we performed our fitness regimens. Their training reflected the activities on most military bases. Usually there would be several groups, some large and some small, running in different areas of the campus. I could tell the fast group. It was usually smaller and normally passed me at a full gait. They wouldn't be singing cadence like other groups; they would just be running hard and sweating profusely. Then there were groups who sang or chanted as they ran in formation. The group leader would go back and encourage the runners who were falling behind. When I was in the military, we would refer to that as "picking up the stragglers." I had been a straggler during basic training. Then, as a drill sergeant, I'd often pick up the stragglers. Once a soldier always a soldier, and I desperately wanted to join in and have some fun. It wasn't easy, but I restrained myself.

One day, however, during one of our close encounters, I made it known that I was retired from the military. Soon after that, some of them would shout, "Top of the morning, Sergeant!" or incorporate me into their songs—"Look to your right, and what do you see? Another old soldier trying to be like me." I always felt proud when the acknowledged me.

I continued to enjoy exercising, but instead of getting fit, I begin to get tired more easily. *Maybe I'm doing too much*, I thought, so I decreased the number of days and amount of time I tried to exercise. Still, I didn't feel up to par. Knowing what I had been through, especially Mama's death, I thought maybe it was just depression and that it would pass. I did mention it to my doctor, but I did not appreciate her response. She categorized me as in the obese range and insisted that was the cause of my fatigue.

Now that's a stretch, I thought. Immediately, in my defense, I said, "Maybe I'm just big boned. You should check my body fat percentage."

"That's not necessary. I encourage you to lose at least twenty pounds."

I tried, but my head and heart ached as I mentally pushed myself. I just did not feel well. It always felt like I was coming down with the flu. Something about my health didn't feel right. I kept complaining to my doctor, but she always insisted everything looked normal except my blood pressure, and I was on medication for that.

Then, on Mother's Day, she called me. Yes, Mother's Day. All I could think was, *This must be serious*.

She had requested x-rays of my lower back because I complained that it hurt if I stepped a certain way. I wasn't really concerned at that time. I had been in the military, and I expected there might be damage. Her reaction, however, made me very concerned. She told me she'd gotten the results from my x-rays, and there was immense damage to my bones.

"There are tiny fractures all over your body. I want you to see a physiatrist."

I did not understand that term, but instead of asking her, I looked it up. A physiatrist, as it turned out, is a physician who diagnoses and treats acute and chronic pain associated with musculoskeletal conditions. *Wow*, I thought as I read the definition.

Waiting for my appointment with the physiatrist provoked panic. I had often ignored or pushed through my pain. Now, I faced the possibility that putting my health aside might have major consequences. For the next few weeks, I felt anxious. I prayed to God that my life choices had not been detrimental. The last thing I wanted to hear from a doctor was, "If we had just found it sooner …"

When I finally met the specialist, I was relieved to know that my condition was not quite what I had considered. There was, however, extensive damage to my bones, especially hips and back. It was primarily osteoarthritis, but there were some bone spurs and bulging discs. This was classified as *degenerative disc disease*, and it basically comes from wear and tear due to aging. I wasn't that old, but being a soldier had to be taken in to consideration, especially the fact that I was thirty-three when I decided to become a drill sergeant. I asked if that made me feel so tired.

He acknowledged that it could contribute to fatigue and that it was not going to get better. "We'll just monitor progression, and try to keep the inflammation under control for now," he explained. He prescribed a medication for pain and inflammation. He gave me some guidelines that included stretching, walking, and water therapy. He was specific, however, that there was to be no running. "Your days of pounding on pavement are over. Also, no heavy lifting, pulling, or reaching. You should not contribute to the deterioration in any way. You must learn to take life nice and easy now."

This was a blow to the ego of a "no-limit soldier" but also a blessing.

It would contribute to my effort of redefining myself. I had learned to look for God's way of putting me on the path he wanted me to take. So I incorporated the recommended adjustments and continued my quest to redefine myself.

I was excited about water therapy, so I joined a fitness center with a therapy pool. Entering the water was delightful. I noticed the benefits immediately. It was warm to my body and calming to my spirit. I created a pool routine that included a warm-up, walking, and yoga. What I enjoyed most, however, was floating on my back. It literally took all the weight off my body, and my joints really appreciated that. I went early in the morning when there was hardly anyone there. I could float effortlessly around the pool. It felt like being suspended in midair. I just lay there, meditating and talking to God as the warm water soothed my body.

This soon became my favorite place to be. I was thankful for the recommendation, but the medication was creating another problem. I often had a sick feeling in my stomach, and even the thought of breakfast food made me sick. Eggs, grits, meat in the morning—yuck. I would usually skip breakfast. Now I had to eat before taking the pills in the morning and evening. I had to find something that would not make me sick. Finally, I tried peanut butter on toasted wheat bread and a banana, and it worked. I could take my medication.

Still, it seemed that every few weeks, something needed adjusting. Either I noticed something, or my tests revealed something. My blood pressure was the hardest to control. I had lost about twenty pounds, but my blood pressure was still out of range. Altering my mind-set was the most difficult. I had become accustomed to pushing through whatever was bothering me, physically and mentally, and now that wasn't so easy. I was making the necessary adjustments to every part of my life, but I was becoming increasingly frustrated. I had finally reached the stage of my life where I could focus on my personal goals, but all these health issues were preventing it.

I knew that for a woman of my age, things start to change physically. My changes, however, seemed excessive. I had issues with my bones, nausea, restlessness, blood pressure, anxiety, depression— and the list was growing.

During one of my medical appointments, my doctor got frustrated and said, "You just have so much going on."

It brought me to tears. "I didn't ask for these health problems," I replied.

That led to a testy exchange, after which we each apologized and agreed to discuss the matter. We were both frustrated. I wanted her to fix me, and she couldn't.

"All I can do," she explained, "is try to manage each ailment without complicating the others."

I understood her position and respected her very much. Still, limitation upon limitation weighed heavily on me, like cement, and it was exhausting. Something was making me feel like an old woman, and we had to keep searching for answers. Mama was eighty when she passed, and even though she hadn't done any exercise in years, overall, she was healthy. I seemed to have more health issues than she'd had, and I was only fifty-seven. It was obvious to me that the military had taken its toll. Pushing myself, physically and mentally, was required at the time, but eventually there were consequences, and they were rapidly being revealed.

My doctor ordered test after test. I took every test she suggested, including the one for HIV. That was an awful experience. It took two weeks for the results, and during that time, I considered every possible exposure. Ten years was the test range, and that was a long time to consider every sexual encounter. I was horrified as I explored not the people but the times I'd been exposed. I researched everything about HIV and AIDS, as I sought relief from the anxiety I felt. Finally, she called me to schedule an appointment for the results. My knees got weak, and my hands began to tremble, despite the fact that she told me not to assume anything negative. The results simply could not be given over the phone.

The test revealed no exposure. I was so relieved, but the experience enlightened me to many things about the disease and dispelled many rumors. Most important, it emphasized the importance of being more responsible.

After months of evaluations, I eventually was diagnosed with Gulf War syndrome. This diagnosis included a list of unexplainable medical issues. Chronic fatigue syndrome (CFS) was a part of that list, and so was muscle and joint pain. I had been in Saudi Arabia during the Gulf War, and this was a common diagnosis among those veterans. Chemical exposure was identified as the more likely culprit. I didn't doubt being exposed to something over there. Everything was in the air—sand from sandstorms, smoke from burning urine, and eventually the smoke from oil-well fires. During one period, the skies were so dark it looked like night in the middle of the day. Chemical alarms sounded constantly, and there was no way our protective masks were completely effective. Between the sand and sweat on my face, my mask rarely stayed sealed tightly, suctioned against my skin, as required. Thinking back to my health immediately after returning from the Gulf War, I realized there were signs that something was wrong. I'd gone to several doctors and specialists because I kept feeling sick. I was referred to an endocrinologist, who stated there was nothing to explain all the changes in my body.

There was no cure for this diagnosis, and it was not easy to accept living the rest of my life with these limitations. I continued to limit my activities to a minimum. My days of walking five miles, washing the car, and cutting the grass—even cooking big meals—were over. Mentally, all the adjustments left me feeling inadequate. It was hard relinquishing the Superwoman mentality of which I'd always been so proud.

4

The Superwoman Mentality

I was often referred to as a superwoman. I was always flattered because while the military gave me most of the training, I knew God had given me my cape, and I did all things through Christ, who strengthened me. The term *superwoman* has been widely used to describe strong women, meant to pay homage to their ability to survive any obstacle.

Many women I knew performed amazing juggling acts just to keep their worlds from falling apart. Multitasking was a normal requirement as they tried to raise their children and work full-time jobs. The men's roles seemed minimal in comparison. Even if they were providers, rarely did they also do the grocery shopping, cook the food, run to the school, and all the other tasks associated with managing the home. In many cases, men were not even present. Nevertheless, the responsibilities had to be fulfilled, and there was no time to waste with complaining. *Just keep going, and things will lighten up eventually*—that was the attitude I had.

Remarkably, every role I was obligated to perform involved extreme circumstances. At the age of two, I learned to adapt to the loss of my father. Then I had to adapt to an abusive childhood. By age twenty I was raising my three children. Finally, I met the man who loved me, married me, and became a vital part of the family.

After ten years, he was diagnosed with cancer, and after caring for him for eighteen months, he died from the disease. I was devastated. Then, one year later, my eighteen-month-old granddaughter died in a car accident.

Despite my unwavering faith, I spent many years angry and confused. I tried desperately to understand why bad things kept happening. Why was my childhood filled with so many negative memories? Why did my dad, my brother, my husband, and my granddaughter all die so young and so tragically? Why did my only sister become an addict? I needed her; I needed my sister. I was a strong woman, and I was determined to survive, but now I was sick. All these issues constantly swirled around in my head.

"Why, Lord, why?" I asked God. As if God wasn't aware, I ranted about who I was and how I'd lived my life thus far. "I try to live according to your guidance. I raised my children the best I could. I pushed through all my fears and pains and ignored most personal interests and desires. I set the best example I could. I've been a good daughter. I've been a good sister. I was a good wife, but now my husband is gone, and I'm a single parent again. I was also a good soldier. I followed all the rules and maintained the highest level of discipline at all times. Yet repeatedly I have been kicked like I was nothing. Each time I was compelled to take the high road, to turn the other cheek. Why, Father? Why must I endure so much hardship? I just don't understand. It all seems so unfair."

I asked God *why* many times before and received answers during different situations. I always believed and trusted that God was in control of my life. At this point, however, my frustration was overwhelming, and I needed to understand. Once again, I asked God why, and this is what he spoke to my spirit:

"I have given you everything you needed for every battle. I gave you rest before and after. I kept you calm and protected you from harm. I gave you the strength and wisdom to endure. You are frustrated because you keep looking back and try to keep a tally of every bad experience. Each time you ask forgiveness for your sins, I wipe your slate clean. You must do the same with past events. Then you will have peace."

Words cannot explain the intensity of this message. It was astounding. Immediately after receiving the message, I saw a flash of Lot's wife in the Bible as she was turned into a pillar of salt for looking back. It was as if God had to provide me with an illustration of the consequences of looking back. Thinking about it still causes me to tremble.

Despite my life-changing revelation, the impact of past events on my life could not be denied—primarily, the fact that I could never focus on my greatest ambitions. I always had to stay focused on the battle at hand. As a result, time after time I ignored my own health, wealth, and social desires. Through it all, however, in the back of my mind, there was always a vision. I was constantly thinking about how to completely transform myself—mind, body, and soul. I wanted to become a writer. I wanted to dress to impress, have a social calendar, travel, sip fine wine, and socialize with ambitious people. While those desires were never lost, they had been suppressed for a very long time, and this would be no easy feat. It would take every skill I possessed or could acquire to go from superwoman, always engaged in battle, to Cinderella at the ball.

Yet I could hear Mama from heaven saying, "Go enjoy your life!" And she was right; the time was now. If I didn't try my best to make this transformation, this most likely would be the place in my life where I'd look back with the most regret. I still had that superwoman mentality, but I knew God was ordering my steps. He was making it clear; it was time for a softer, gentler lifestyle. I marveled at the likelihood that God had taken away my superwoman cape just as surely as he had given it to me.

I saw a quote that fueled my determination to become a brand-new me. It was, "Life isn't about finding yourself. Life is about creating yourself." Those few words spoke volumes and made my desire to transform myself seem possible.

5

All Dressed Up with Nowhere to Go

As a child, I didn't have a closet filled with nice clothes. I don't even remember having a Barbie with different outfits. Nor do I remember wearing hair bows or having that polished look like some girls. Except for Easter and Christmas, I never felt refined. As I got older, I always had to be creative, and while that helped to build my character, it didn't enhance my feminine side. I dreamed of having a closet filled with outfits for every occasion. By the time I was old enough to do something about it, I was pregnant. I did the best I could with my little girls, but I was off to the military by the time my oldest turned five. Throughout my years of parenting and soldiering, it was all about convenience. I had to dress ready for action, so braids were usually the choice for me and my daughters. Lately, it had been about comfort, so I was usually in sweats and workout shoes. I always dressed like I was ready to do something physical.

Now, with all that behind me, I had a choice, and I wanted to get rid of that image. I wanted to dress up, all the way up. I wanted to look soft, feminine, and more like a lady. I wanted a nice haircut and my face made up like a beauty queen's. I wanted to wear soft, pretty dresses and high-heeled shoes, which were against doctor's advice. I'd keep that in mind, but it was time to go shopping.

When I got to the department store, immediately I requested the assistance of the sales lady. I knew if I shopped for myself, I would end up with much of the same thing I already had in my closet. After our introduction, I explained that I was trying to change my image, and if it wasn't soft, I didn't want it. The sales lady worked closely with me. One thing she emphasized was color.

"What colors do you like to wear?" she asked.

"Oh, I usually wear earth tones, mainly black, gray, brown."

"Really?" she replied. "Those colors are fine if you accentuate them properly, but girl, you need some color in your life." We both laughed. "You want to wear bright colors—colors that say you're alive and happy!"

I left the store with several new outfits. I also got shoes, a purse, and jewelry to match my new attire. I wanted to be able to look in my closet and pick an entire outfit to wear, not my usual method of scrambling through drawers, trying this and that, until I had mounds of clothes on the bed, floor, and everywhere. I was satisfied with most of the pieces she had chosen. They were not too extreme. *But I don't know how I let her talk me into that orange sweater dress*, I thought. I hadn't loss that much weight. I looked like a pumpkin. *Maybe my daughter will like it*, I thought. *If not, it'll just be in there with all the other failed attempts.* I simply hated to take things back for exchange. Eventually, they'd just make it onto my Goodwill pile, several pieces of which still had the tags on them.

Now with my wardrobe a little softer, I needed to do something different with my hair. Again, braids were usually my preference. Finding a beautician had always been a problem for me—a major problem. I'd gone to many different stylists in different states, and it was always a memorable experience. *I mean, for God's sake, did you really start on my head at one o'clock, and it's eleven, and you're still not done?* Once I was in the midst of this ordeal, I had no choice but to continue with it. Nonetheless, no hairstyle should take ten hours. I've watched in the mirror as two African girls performed synchronized hair braiding. There was one on each side, and they were braiding so fast, it looked like they were playing Double Dutch on my head.

Once I went to a reputable salon, famous for cutting any kind of hair. When I saw the different customers, I felt sure it was the perfect place for me. It was a full-service salon, and I needed a perm, wrap, and flat iron. I got the attention of one of the black stylists, thinking she would be more familiar with black hair and would do the best job—big mistake. When she applied the perm and started combing through it, over and over and over, I knew she was lacking Hair Care 101. She finally finished and boasted about how silky it was. As soon as I was driving home, I knew it was overprocessed. I could smell the odor of burned hair. I was livid. I called my daughter Tynisha and ranted about the experience.

She asked who it was, and then said she knew the girl. "Oh, I could have told you not to go to her. She does good cuts, but that's all. She is not good at hair care."

"What? How is that even possible? She works in a freaking shop that requires her to do it all. This is absolutely ridiculous."

"Just go back there," she said.

"For what? What are they going to do?"

"Well, at least they will know she overprocessed it and make sure she doesn't do it again."

"No, they should know the abilities of their stylists before they hire them, not let them figure it out."

So for the past year, I'd been wearing a sew-in hair weave. I'd take it out, wash and condition it, and put it back in braids. Then I'd sew the weave back in. I kept the ends clipped, so once all the overprocessed hair was gone, I had a full head of natural hair. My son suggested that I wear it natural, as that was one of the current styles. Sure, I was proud of my African American heritage, but I hated my hair short and nappy. It just did not work for me. I wanted a mild perm and a few layers. I could wrap and flat iron my own hair, so it would be easy for me to manage. I went to a major department store that had a full-service salon, and they did an excellent job. My hair had so much body. It felt silky, and it made me look and feel sexy. I was improving my image, and people were starting to notice, so I continued.

My nails were next on my agenda. I decided to try a new shop in the area. People were raving about it because they served wine during the appointments. When I entered, the first thing I noticed was the difference in nail technicians. They were of all nationalities, male and female. After I was seated, I was offered a glass of wine.

"Red or white?" the lady asked.

"Red, please."

"Okay, your technician will be with you shortly."

The atmosphere was very relaxing. Bamboo décor, green plants, and works of art provided a Zen effect. There were flat-screen televisions throughout, but soft music was the only sound I could hear. The attendant returned with my wine and reminded me that I could have another at no charge. "Very impressive," I replied. *Now this is my idea of a nail shop*, I thought as I basked in the atmosphere.

My technician, a black girl, soon came, and she was very professional. I got a full set of acrylic nails. I wanted them as short as possible. I really didn't like fake nails, but if they were natural, I would bite them off. I'd been biting my nails for as long as I could remember. It was a habit I had not been able to break. I also got a pedicure, which would take me a long time to do comfortably on my own. Military boots had done a number on my feet, and I never felt comfortable about people seeing them. Finally, after witnessing so much devastation from war, I became thankful that I still had my feet, no matter how ugly they were. I chose a chocolate-red nail polish, and it matched my skin tone very well. The wine, massage chair, and foot massage relaxed me on every level, and there was no doubt I would return.

When I was growing up, I was often referred to as a natural beauty. I had a caramel skin and light-brown eyes. I never had to wear much makeup. But that was forty years ago. Life had certainly caused a few changes, and I needed to put on a little makeup if I wanted to look my best. I decided to get some lashes because everyone was wearing them, and I thought they'd look nice. I went to a place in the local mall that specialized in lashes and brows. When I walked in, I was surprised by the different options. Full-sized face shots emphasized the many different lash styles and eyebrow shapes. Like my mother, I had skimpy eyebrows, but I was not bold enough to just cut those off and draw new ones each day, as she had done. I usually used my mascara brush to build thicker ones.

"May I help you, ma'am?" the Asian lady asked with a big, bright smile.

"Oh, hi," I replied. "I love your kimono."

"Thank you," she said softly as she bowed her head down and then back up. "You want lashes today?"

"Well, this will be my first time, so I'm not sure."

"Oh, come, I do nice lash for you. Not too much for first time."

"Okay," I replied. "I trust you."

"Oh, yeah, yeah, you trust me. I take good care of you."

As soon as she tried to touch my eye, I knew there was going to be a problem.

"Close eye. Keep eye closed. Be very still."

My eyeball was doing a dance and screaming, *Wait! Don't touch me!*

"You very nervous for first time, yeah?"

"Yes, ma'am."

"You have to stay very still. Look down and to your right. Don't close too tight." Then I heard, "Oh, no," as she removed the lash she had just placed. After messing up several times, I could hear her frustration. "Ma'am, you must be very still."

"OK, just stop," I said. "I'm sorry; I just can't do it. How much do I owe you for trying?"

"Oh, no charge for that. You come back; try next time."

"Okay. Thank you very much."

Now that's a darn shame, I thought as I walked out the shop. *I can't even get lashes. Oh well, back to my old method. I'll just have to build my own.*

I stopped and got a good primer and mascara and then headed home. I had everything I needed—new outfit, new cut, new nails, and makeup. I was ready to put it all together. I put on some jazz music, ran a nice bubble bath, and poured a glass of Cabernet Sauvignon. Google voice taught me how to pronounce the name of the wine, and I loved to say it. I felt like a wine connoisseur, when all I'd previously known was red and white, sweet or not so sweet. I didn't know what wine went with what meal, but I knew that was soon going to change.

I relaxed in a warm bubble bath, sipping wine and enjoying my music. I got out and lavished myself with cocoa-butter lotion. I made sure every sexy inch of my body was covered. This was known to be a healing lotion for many years, and I needed to replenish moisture and even my skin tone. I rubbed and rubbed as if things were going to happen faster if I got it deep into my skin. Finally, I slipped on a short silk nightie and went to the mirror. I kept the scarf on my hair as I cleansed and moisturized my face.

I took my time and put on my foundation and blush. I used a bit more than normal because I wanted a dramatic look. I put on blue eye shadow because I'd read that blue made brown eyes pop. Then I started building my lashes. I applied the primer and then carefully brushed on several coats of mascara. It took a while, but I had a nice-looking set of lashes, and I was very proud. I took off the scarf and unwrapped and loosened my hair with my fingers. It fell right into place, and so did my new look. I slipped on my calypso pants and sexy new blouse. Fuchsia was a very nice color and went well with the hint of fuchsia in the pants. My strappy sandals had a wedge heel, not too high. The time might come for high heels, and I was looking forward to it. But for now, I needed to be comfortable. *Wow*, I thought as I looked at myself in the mirror. It was an astonishing transformation, if I did say so myself. For the next few weeks, I went through this ritual over and over, sometimes two or three wardrobe changes a day, just to find that look. But the sad thing was, I got all dressed up but had nowhere to go.

My days of backyard barbecues had to be minimized. I didn't want to sweat or swipe at mosquitoes. I'd spent many days in that type of setting, and I'd enjoyed it immensely. I loved to play Spades—that was a favorite option for most of the people I grew up with. At this stage of my life, however, I needed comfort. I wanted to go out to dinner, not prepare it. I wanted to be entertained, not be the entertainment. Finally, I had the option of going to events that created the atmosphere I preferred.

People in the military came from all around the world, and their personalities and upbringings influenced their décor and ideas for entertainment, as did mine. So there was a variety of social settings I was privy to as a soldier. The military itself, however, exposed me to the most elegant settings. As my rank increased, so did my invitations to special events. For those events, we were usually required to wear our dress uniforms, and sometimes this formal attire was the only option. Regardless, I always felt like a queen at those occasions, and that greatly influenced my desire to feel that way more often.

Now, I simply did not have a social life. I wasn't dating, and my life had been strictly business for years. I was making the effort to change that, but I had to be careful. I didn't like idle chatter or loose talk anymore. I preferred being engaged in well-informed, dignified conversations. There had to be a touch of class.

6

Moth to a Social Flame

If I watched another police drama on TV, I felt I was going to scream. I wanted to go out—somewhere—and I had no clue where to start. There were many challenges for middle-aged women, and a place to socialize with people of our age and maturity level was one of them. I wanted to find a place I could go and have a glass of wine, listen to some jazz, maybe dance a little, and meet new people. But where in this town could I go? There were places I could go for happy hour, but by nine the young crowd would take over. My children and several grandchildren were old enough to go to clubs. And so were the young people I had been supervising over the past seven years. Seeing them in a club would quickly take me out of relaxation mode and put me back into mentoring mode.

More important, I was no longer a juke-joint kind of girl. I wanted to be dressed in a nice cocktail gown and go out with an escort who knew how to be a gentleman. We'd have a few cocktails, listen to the music, and enjoy each other's company. Afterward, we could have dinner in a nice restaurant; where I had to use a knife and fork. *I can eat ribs and chicken wings with my fingers*, I told myself, *and even collard greens and cornbread with no problem, but on a date, fine dining is my preference.* All things considered, my options were limited.

Once again, I was at a point in my life where I realized I could get stuck. There was the strong possibility that the social life I wanted was not going to happen. I supposed I could just settle in and do what everyone else was doing. Maybe that's what had happened to Mama. She would often say, "When I was young ..." And she would always urge me to go out and enjoy myself. I could tell it was from a deeply personal perspective. For the last twenty-plus years of her life, however, Mama had been satisfied being in her house. She'd lost interest in shopping, visiting friends, or any outside entertainment long ago. She had become content to cook or do her crafts. Often, she'd call me to say she'd tried a new recipe and wanted me to taste it. Many times, in response, I'd say I'd made something—"I'll bring you some when I come over." We were proud of our homemaking skills, but we each wanted more.

Mama didn't specifically say what she'd dreamed of becoming or when those dreams changed. Yet remnants of her desires were reflected in her expensive taste. She only wanted name-brand items. It was so out of budget that most of her close family commented on her choices. They didn't seem to understand, but I understood completely. I would rather buy one expensive item than several cheap ones. Even the foods she prepared were displayed with a touch of elegance. The dish was presented attractively on a plate, platter, or bowl, accented with parsley, sliced fruit, or some other garnish. That style and flair was undeniable for both of us. When Mama reached a place where she accepted her inability to make it happen, she still urged me to do so.

At this point, I wanted a social life, I needed a social life, and I was going to have a social life. This wasn't about dating; it was about dressing up and going out to explore the world. It was about learning new dances, tasting fine wines, and eating foods that needed an introduction. I also wanted to attend musicals and concerts. I kept thinking of all the things that had inspired me in New York City, and I was becoming restless. I sat down and considered my options. I wanted to build a social calendar. After pondering several events, I decided that church was a good place to start, especially since I had not attended regularly in years. I loved the Lord and I respected the church, but it had become uncomfortable to me. There was just too much going on. I needed a place to worship where it was quiet, just me and the Lord.

Often, I'd just turn on contemporary Christian music and meditate on the words. Sometimes the Spirit would come over me so strong, and I'd get so filled with emotions that tears would flow freely, and I'd just praise God right there in my room. Then Joel Osteen became the messenger. It seemed like every sermon he preached was written and delivered just for me, directly to me. My relationship with the Lord was powerful and unyielding, but I also understood the need to fellowship with other Christians. Attending church needed to become a weekly event. I could watch my televangelists early and then go to church.

So on my calendar I filled in, *church on Sundays*. Toastmasters was another event I wanted to attend but kept putting off. The organization was world renowned, and I wanted to learn as much as I could about public speaking and fine tune those skills. The schedule posted on their website indicated meetings on the first and third Mondays at six o'clock in the evening, so I added that to my calendar.

Movies were a good option once or twice a month, so I added it to the calendar. The events I had on my schedule could be attended without a companion, and that was great. I hoped I would meet people with whom I wanted to socialize. I did have one cousin, Sarah Elice, with whom I met regularly. She insisted on being called by her first and middle names. She said her middle name was Italian and made her feel glamorous. Sarah Elice was different from many people her age. She was in her early thirties, but she had an old-fashioned kind of innocence. We'd meet at a restaurant of our choice, have a big salad, and laugh and talk about life. She didn't engage in gossip or mess, but she had a mean streak, and if you messed with one of her boys, you would see that mean streak quickly. She and I were very close, so I put her name with a question mark on Tuesdays, until I made sure that day was good for her.

I was still yearning to get out of town to a lounge or club, but I was reluctant, especially since I wasn't dating anyone. I just wanted to dance. I explored the option of driving to a military base and staying for the weekend. Surely, Huntsville or Montgomery had a place for soldiers to socialize. There would be very little chance of running into my offspring or anyone else I knew. I neatly wrote "Weekend getaway (destination to be determined)" on the first weekend of the month. Unfortunately, when I checked, neither base had the social settings I expected, and that option went unfulfilled. There were two colleges in the area, and they often had activities, so I put "Events on campus (to be determined)." I also noted "Weddings and other special events, as invited." Soon, I had a monthly calendar of social events for consideration, and I was ready to implement my plans.

I followed my social calendar, and everything went great. I stayed on my daily fitness regimen. I'd listen to Joel Osteen early, and then I'd go to church on Sunday mornings. I usually had lunch with Sarah Elice once a week. Still missing, however, was my desire to go dancing. For that, I needed a partner.

7

Hidden Treasure Trove

The lack of interesting males in my area was frustrating. I had been in the military, surrounded by men, for over fifteen years, and dating never had been a problem. There were males interested in me, but I did not feel any spark for them. Honestly, what I really wanted in a mate was no longer clear. At age sixteen, I just wanted him to look like the Marlborough man in the cigarette commercial—light skin with dark hair and mustache. When I had my children, the need for physical attraction was no longer important. One specific question determined if I should date someone: "Can I trust him around my children?" I had dated over the years, and no matter how much I liked someone, I would let him go if I didn't trust him around my children.

My own childhood set the standards for how my children would be raised. There was no textbook on how to specifically raise each individual child, but I believed it was most important for them to be happy and free, especially at home. So when the man I dated seemed more concerned with partying, washing his car every time it got a spot, or spending every dime on expensive tennis shoes, he was not the man for me. I was a mother, and my primary concern was for my children.

That's why people close to me were shocked when I said no to K. C., the love of my life, but married George, my total opposite. No one could understand my decision. K. C. and I looked good together and shared love together, but he was obsessed with the social scene. At that time, I needed a family man. George loved me, and he adored my children. I trusted him with them. Soon, we had a son together and became a happy family. After his death, I again raised them as a single parent. Now a single woman with grown children, I honestly did not know what I wanted in a man. It was time to reevaluate.

I researched "how to get back into the dating scene," and I considered every option. I wanted someone who shared my interests or who had interests I wanted to share. Now could I examine his qualities without opening myself up too much. I just needed to explore; I didn't want to date numerous men. Internet dating was the option I found most intriguing, so I set up a profile on a free site. For me, this was instant gratification. I strolled through page after page of men, reading their profiles, laughing out loud at some and totally disgusted by others. I wasn't personally offended, but I sincerely doubted that I would ever date anyone from the site.

But I quickly discovered the deeper values of having so much information at hand. This was useful information, and I could use it to my advantage. I'd read the profiles of men and women. I looked at the pictures of men and women. I was making assessments of the things I liked or didn't like about the men. I compared myself to the women to see if I could identify characteristics that would enhance me personally. Day after day, I searched and researched. I said hi to some and replied if prompted. Some days it seemed useless—ridiculous even; still, I continued to explore.

Examining the profiles became a fascination for me. I wasn't particularly looking for a date; it was just amusing. Some of the profile names made me laugh out loud. Some were cute and clever, but some were downright illegal ("Comsitonmyface"? Really?) But most amusing were the photos. One man had a shotgun, and he was in a shooting stance that just cracked me up. He looked as though he was taking direct aim at the camera and with such intensity I wanted to take cover. "Exactly who is he trying to attract? Annie Oakley?" Then there were those guys whose poses were so sexy it was sad. Those pictures screamed, "I want to have sex," or maybe "Look at me;

I'm having sex." I was always amused. I had great respect for their freedom of expression, but sometimes I was taken by surprise.

I started to realize this was my company. Every evening, I turned on my computer, and someone wanted to chat with me. Some were nice guys who just wanted to say they liked my profile. I had been doing this for over a year, and I had never gone out with anyone.

Then one day, a guy from my area asked me out for dinner. I felt that the area he suggested was safe, so I agreed to meet him there. He was a very nice-looking guy and appeared to be respectful. But as soon as we walked in the door of the restaurant, and I heard people call his name, I felt uncomfortable. *Is this the place where he brings all his dates?* I wondered. We sat and talked, and I was not impressed. The conversation got too deep too fast. Immediately, he started talking about his ex-girlfriends and why they'd broken up, his money problems, and his children. Everything was so negative, and he was quite arrogant.

Then, finally, the food came. After he had eaten half of his steak, he complained that it wasn't cooked as he'd wanted. He got loud with the waiter, and I was totally turned off. He did not handle that situation properly. It was our first date, and he was making a scene. After we walked out, he walked me to my car and tried to hold my hand. We said our goodbyes, and he tried to kiss me. I was flabbergasted. I was sure that would be my last date with someone from a dating site.

Still, I enjoyed the site and had become friendly with some there, and we talked regularly. Through those conversations, I learned of the risks some had taken with people they'd met online. One guy told of his relationship and said he had been ripped off. He'd taken out someone a few times, and they really liked each other. Things were going great, and after only a few months, she moved in with him. One day he came home from work, and there was no furniture in the house. She had taken everything he had, and law enforcement could not locate her. He said he was devastated, yet he was still on the site.

I heard similar stories from men and women, but I was not afraid. I felt safe, as long as I was in the comfort of my own home. This became such a habit for me that if I was off for a day or so, they'd ask where I'd been, and I did the same with several guys. Occasionally, girls would contact me to say they liked my profile or a picture. Then there was "Sweet Machoho," who made it clear that if I ever decided to join the "family" (LGBT), I should look her up. That was not what I was expecting, but it was a dating site. Everyone was exploring the options. I knew I would date again someday, but I was willing to wait rather than rush and end up with the headaches of a bad relationship.

Late one night, as I lay across the bed, casually scrolling through the matches the company suggested, one guy jumped out at me. He was cute—not flashy, not too over the top. I read his profile, and it made me smile. I kept reading and looking at his pictures. For the first time, I felt a connection. I liked him. I thought about it over and over. Finally, I had to say hello.

8

Funtyme 911

Zena	Hello.
FT911	Hello, Zena, how are you?
Zena	I'm good. I'd prefer you call me Karah. That's actually my name.
FT911	Nice to meet you. Karah. My name is Mitchell, but I prefer Mitch … "Funtyme 911."
Karah	Nice to make your acquaintance, Mitch. I just wanted to say hi. Got to get some sleep. Early wake up. Have a good night.
Mitch	You too, love. TTYL. "Funtyme 911."
Mitch	Good morning, love! … "Funtyme 911."
Karah	Hey, Mitch … I was just looking at your profile.
Mitch	Good, because I've been looking at yours all night. Hardly slept at all. "Funtyme 911."
Karah	Why is "Funtyme 911" on your replies?
Mitch	LOL … That's just my tagline. It automatically appears after I write. I was just exploring, and honestly, now I can't figure out how to take it off … "Funtyme 911."
Karah	Interesting. Well, I can't help you, but I think it's kind of cute.

Mitch   Cool. Hope your day is super! TTYL.

Karah   Hello, where is my friend? I feel like crap.

Mitch   Hey, love, busy day. Are you feeling better? … "Funtyme 911."

Karah   Yes, thanks, upset stomach. I'll be fine. How are you?

Mitch   I'm super, rolling through Missouri enjoying my music! "Funtyme 911."

Karah   Are you driving and texting me? Please be safe.

Mitch   Now that's sweet. No, boo. It's all voice activated … "Funtyme 911."

We exchanged phone numbers then, and he asked if he could call. I was a little nervous when my cell phone rang. I cleared my throat and enthusiastically said hello.

"Hello. How are you, Ms. Karah?"

"I am wonderful, and how are you?"

"I am excited about getting to know you better"

"Great. So am I."

"Hope we can make plans to meet soon."

"Maybe."

"OK, nice hearing your voice. I'll text you later. I'll always text before I call to make sure it's a good time, and I prefer you do the same. I'm interrupted a lot by this CB radio and must respond quickly."

"I understand; no problem. Sounds good to me."

We said our goodbyes, and I had to sit back and sigh. *Damn, he has a sexy voice.* Then, I didn't hear from him for a few days.

Mitch: Hey love, how are you? "Funtyme 911."

Karah: I'm good. Just hoping that trusting you is not a mistake

Mitch: Let me assure you, I'm a nice guy. I'm very kind and I don't like drama. Can I call you? "Funtyme 911."

Karah: Sure.

"Hey, boo, now tell me more about yourself," Mitch said.

"Well, I am fifty-seven, and writing is my passion. I'm retired now, but I hope to become a respected author. Maybe you'll see me on *Oprah* one day. I love music—all music, even rap. I prefer jeans and boots to dresses and heels, but I am trying to change that. How about you?"

"Oprah, really? I'm scared of you. Don't act like you don't know me when you make the big time. Well, I'm fifty-three, and driving is my passion. I've been driving trucks for fifteen years, and I ride a Harley. I'm divorced and work a lot. What do you write about?"

"I write about life experiences. I may write about you someday. I also like motorcycles. I went to a class to learn to ride. I did okay but haven't ridden since."

"We will have to change that and soon. I ride every chance I get. I'm in a riding club. You must ride with us sometime."

"Of course; just take care of me. I love your sexy voice."

"Thank you. You sound sweet, but I'm not so sure, especially since you are military. Oh, I studied your profile."

That caused me to laugh out loud. "Yes, retired army," I said, "but there is a softer, gentler me these days."

"Good! By the way, I like rap too, but I prefer R&B. And one more thing, I would love to see you in jeans and boots."

"Sure. I think I have nice legs and sometimes I wear very short skirts and dresses."

"I like nice legs. You can send me a photo of you anytime."

"Your voice is soothing. It makes me feel like I want you to hold me."

"Chemistry?" he asked.

"Oh wow! Maybe chemistry, but we are not ready for that. I think we better focus on walking, talking and holding hands."

"Yes," he agreed "I'd like that."

"Really?"

"Yes ... I'd like for us to walk and hold hands. I would love to see you. Maybe tomorrow night? I'm scheduled to have dinner in your area with some club members."

"No, that's too soon for me. I don't want to rush."

"Okay, calm down. I'm not rushing. Take all the time you need."

I laughed again. "I am calm. So tell me, Mitch, how would you like for things to go with us?"

"The sky is the limit with me. But first I would like for us to meet, talk, walk, hold hands, and see where it goes. And you?"

"The same—the sky is the limit."

"Great. Got to get some sleep. Text you tomorrow. Sweet dreams, boo."

"You too. Good night."

Mitch: Good morning sexy! "Funtyme 911."

Karah: GM ... I'm still in bed, and that's not good. I'm usually a morning person.

Mitch: I am also a morning person. "Funtyme 911."

Karah: Good, but today I feel like shit again. No problem, I'll just stay in bed.

Mitch: Must be nice. Hope you feel better soon. I'll be thinking of you. "Funtyme 911."

Karah: There's no reason to be concerned ... I'm not sick, just tired from writing, I guess. I need a few days to rest and reenergize.

Mitch: I wish I was there to spoil you. "Funtyme 911."

Karah: We would spoil each other.

Mitch: I'm kind of busy. Are you going to be able to talk on the phone later? "Funtyme 911"

Karah: Of course.

Mitch: OK, I'll call you in one hour. I need to hear your sexy voice. "Funtyme 911."

Karah: Okay, sweetie.

Our phone conversations were rare and brief. Texting was the primary means of communication because of his job; it was more convenient for both of us. Texting between Mitch and me was different from what I'd experienced before. I remembered texting one of my friends who said, "I don't have time to read all of that. You have to use shortcuts." So I stopped texting her. My grandchildren thought my long texts were funny and couldn't wait to share them with their siblings.

Mitch and I had no problem with spelling out entire words; it made more sense. The few times we did try to shorten words, it took more time trying to explain what it meant. Sometimes I would text him a question, and it would be hours before he could respond. It wasn't like that with me; my schedule was open, and my phone was always close to me, so I could respond right away. I preferred texting. Sometimes I would simply text, "calling."

He usually answered with something sexy, like, "What's on your mind, precious?"

I'd say, "I just wanted to hear that deep, sexy voice."

Texting left a lot to my imagination, and that could be trouble. So while it was intriguing, I realized it could backfire. What if I met him, and he was not what I expected? I started to see a benefit to this internet relationship, and physically meeting Mitch became less and less urgent. Day after day, texting became an obsession. First thing in the morning, I had to look at my phone to make sure I hadn't missed one. Mitch had a crazy work schedule, and sometimes he texted me at two or three in the morning to say, "Thinking of you" or "muah," which was how he spelled the sound of a kiss. The text wouldn't wake me, but I'd respond as soon as I read it.

Throughout the day, I looked forward to hearing the distinct sound of incoming texts.

Mitch: Hey boo, What kind of work did you say you do. "Funtyme 911."

Karah: I told you I don't work. I'm retired. When I feel like it, I work on my books.

Mitch: Nice. Can't wait until I have those options. Why aren't you dating? I'm sure guys come on to you all the time. "Funtyme 911."

Karah: Yeah, but it takes someone very special to impress me.

Mitch: Okay, love, just got off. About to take a shower and get some sleep. Wish you were here. "Funtyme 911."

Karah: Hm. LOL. TTYL.

Mitch: Good morning my new friend. "Funtyme 911."

Karah: Good morning.

Mitch: Now what was that you said about guys not impressing you? "Funtyme 911."

Karah: I am retired from the military. I've been around men a lot. Nice, fit, hardworking, good-looking men, so it's not that easy to impress me.

           Let's talk more about it later, I'm writing; need to stay focused. TTYL.

Mitch: Cool. Wishing you the best on your book. "Funtyme 911."

Karah: Hey, sweetie, I'm free now. Thank you. I'm trying hard to break through as a respected author, and sometimes I can't focus, so when I'm in the zone, I need to stay there.

Mitch: I understand, and I'm going to work very hard at winning some of your time, boo-boo. "Funtyme 911."

Karah: Oh, how sweet.

Mitch: You are special to me already. I want you, got to have you. "Funtyme 911."

Mitch: If you want me to be, I'd love to be your special friend. "Funtyme 911."

Karah:	Ah, slow down, Funtyme. LOL. TTYL.
Mitch:	LOL. Okay, love … "Funtyme 911."
Karah:	Morning, Mitch.
Mitch:	Hey, boo … "Funtyme 911."
Karah:	I don't know how to feel about these vibes I'm getting.
Mitch:	Good vibes, I hope. Tell me now before my feelings get any deeper … "Funtyme 911."
Karah:	Yeah, the vibes are good. I like you …
Mitch:	I'm glad you like me 'cause I'm really feeling you. "Funtyme 911."
Karah:	We need to talk about these feelings. I felt lonely all night. I wanted to kiss you.
Mitch:	OMG, I'm a very, very good kisser, so be careful. You will want another and another. "Funtyme 911."
Karah:	LOL. I am not afraid, but one minute I want to kiss you; next minute it feels so forbidden.
Mitch:	Talking is cool, but when we meet, things will become much clearer. "Funtyme 911."
Mitch:	We can take one day at a time, and if you don't like me, I'll go away. "Funtyme 911."
Karah:	I think I like the more aggressive you.
Mitch:	What? Which one? "Funtyme 911."
Karah:	The one who wants me, got to have me.
Mitch:	Oh no, can't tell you that too much. I don't want to scare you off. "Funtyme 911."
Mitch:	We will walk hand in hand at the park and talk I'm old school. "Funtyme 911."
Karah:	I like you … a lot.
Mitch:	Maybe. "Funtyme 911."
Karah:	I do … can't you tell?

Mitch: Kind of, but not like me. I'm feeling you too deep already. "Funtyme 911."

Karah: Keep being sweet. These walls will come down.

Mitch: I want to look in your eyes and hear you say you like me. Then I'll know. "Funtyme 911."

Mitch: Until then I'll be trying to pull you closer and closer to me. "Funtyme 911."

Karah: I can't wait for our first kiss.

Mitch: I don't only kiss on the lips, so I hope you got your big-girl card ... LOL. "Funtyme 911."

Karah: Oh my, if we fall head over heels in love at first sight ... can you handle that?

Mitch: Yes, that will be beautiful. "Funtyme 911."

Mitch: I can't believe you are single, as fly as you are ... No other female has my heart, and I'm hoping you will be the one. "Funtyme 911."

Karah: I'm still wondering about you having enough time for me.

Mitch: Don't worry. I'll blow you away every chance I get, so when I can't be there, you'll have lots of great memories. "Funtyme 911."

Karah: Wow, Good answer. Muah ... have a wonderful day.

Mitch: You too, love ... TTYL. "Funtyme 911."

Texting with Mitch had me salivating like Pavlov's dogs. Even when we weren't working, we texted instead of talking on the phone. I couldn't wait until he was off so we could text each other to sleep. We discussed everything through text, and I would go back and reread them to make sure I didn't miss something important. It was also fulfilling to know he had that kind of time. Surely there couldn't be anyone else taking up much of his time.

However, there were times when I wouldn't hear from him for a couple of days. I couldn't help but think he could have a woman or even a wife with whom who he spent those days. But I didn't let that stop me, nor did I ask him about that possibility. I was just taking him at his word. In time, everything would be revealed. For now, I was just enjoying this new romance. I couldn't wait to curl up in bed and read his texts. My responses were usually quick and fiery. Sometimes he'd say "huh," and I'd have to break down my response. I wasn't playing a game with him; I honestly hoped for a happy ending with us. I hoped he wasn't playing games with me, but if he was, I was fully prepared to exit, stage right, as if it was all part of a performance.

Karah: Ah, clearing my throat.

Mitch: What's up, boo? Crazy day here; miss you. "Funtyme 911."

Karah: Miss you too. TTYL.

Mitch: Good morning, girl of my dreams "Funtyme 911."

Karah: Morning! I missed you yesterday.

Mitch: I missed you too. Things got so busy; plus, it was raining. I just had to keep my head in the game. I fell asleep in the chair with my work clothes on. Woke up around two, missing my boo-boo. But I didn't want to wake you; just got a shower and went back to sleep. "Funtyme 911."

Mitch: How are you? "Funtyme 911."

Karah: I'm good, but I've been thinking about us a lot. I hope we really come together … you for me … me for you. Working to achieve our goals in life.

Mitch: Sounds good to me, boo. "Funtyme 911."

Karah: I haven't dated in two years, and I'm excited that things are going so well. I want to go for the gold … fall in love like teenagers, but …

Mitch: But what? If you're scared, say you're scared. "Funtyme 911."

Karah: No, but the man for me *must* feel the same!

Mitch: Girl, I'll make you feel like you're 25 again. "Funtyme 911."

Karah: If the chemistry between us is right, the sky is the limit for me. Take me there, and I'll take you there.

Mitch: Girlfriend, don't be afraid. We will get better and better and better ... we got this.

Karah: Do you normally date older women?

Mitch: Nope, but I like you, and age doesn't matter. I aim to please you. Just hold on; it's going to be an adventure like no other. "Funtyme 911."

Karah: It sounds like you're about to take me up on your favorite ride. Take care of me ... It's been a while.

Mitch: How long did you say it's been? Two years? Maybe I should be concerned about that? LOL. I'll be very careful, but you must know—my love is like a drug, and you could get addicted. "Funtyme 911."

Karah: No don't say that. Okay ... I'm not ready.

Mitch: OMG. "Funtyme 911."

Karah: You're gonna have me all f ... ed up. I don't want that.

Mitch: What, boo? I'll just hold you, rub on you, kiss you, rub you all over in baby oil, and ... put you to sleep. That's not so bad. I'll start there. "Funtyme 911."

Karah: Sounds dangerous; maybe I'd better keep my distance, and you stay over there.

Mitch: LOL. Girl, you are tripping. "Funtyme 911."

Karah: You will not take care of me ... I will be in trouble. You will be amused at my expense.

Mitch: No, don't think that way. I take love seriously. "Funtyme 911."

Karah: Well, there is that small chance that you'll be the one strung out ... but I will take care of your heart.

Mitch: We'll be fine. Getting strung out together is the only way. "Funtyme 911."

Karah: This is a big step ... I want to take it with you, but I've got to know you've got my best interest in mind.

Mitch: I got you girl, but if you're not ready, don't string me along. "Funtyme 911."

Karah: I won't. I promise.

Mitch: Good. Let's talk tonight. If you like, we can meet up Sunday and take it from there. I'll do whatever you want me to. "Funtyme 911."

Karah: OK. Muah.

Mitch: I sure wish I could get that in person, love! "Funtyme 911."

I fell asleep and missed the text from Mitch, but I had a dream about him that woke up all the sexual sensors throughout my body, and I texted him immediately. From that point on, regardless of whether we texted or talked, sexual innuendo always crept into the conversation.

Karah: Psst! … Mitchell, I miss you.

Mitch: Oh really? No reply to my last text. Guess you were busy. Call me. "Funtyme 911."

"Hey, boo," I said. "Sorry I missed your text. I was having a sexy dream."

"Was it about me?"

"Yep. I can still feel your mouth all over me."

"Damn, that's what's up? Do tell me more."

"You held me all night long."

"Is that all we did?" he asked. "Well, that's only in the dream …"

"I know you can take me there, and I can't wait."

"Neither can I."

"I feel so sexy and a little … moist."

"My imagination is free, and I am enjoying the moment."

"I like you feeling that way." He said.

"I can feel your touch. It's so sensual."

"Oh, my goodness, please go on! he said

"Feel me,...let your imagination take over. My skin is smooth."

"I do feel you boo, he said. this is magical...I am caressing you all over."

"I can feel you. You make me feel so sexy."

"I want to sleep in your arms,"

"Your hands are all over me."

"Okay, I quit."

"Don't stop!" he replied. "You are good."

"No, I'll wait."

"This is going to be extra special when we finally get together, and I can hardly wait. Our love will overflow, and neither of us will be disappointed. That I'm sure of. I really need you, love. I'm going to make you fall in love with me."

"You think so?" I asked. "Then what?"

"You already know. The sky is the limit for us."

"Yes ... I feel you baby."

"Just let it flow."

"Friends ... lovers ... committed lovers ... partners for life ..." I said.

"Wow, Okay, baby. This has been a long night. Let's try to get some rest. That's going to be hard. I need to be there."

"Yes, you do."

"Okay, boo," he said, stifling a yawn. "I do need to get some sleep. I have another long day tomorrow. Good night, love."

"Good night."

Mitch: Good morning, sexy! So when will I see you, boo? "Funtyme 911."

Karah: GM, love. First let me say thank you for reminding me of how beautiful it can be to have the right man in your life. You make me feel like a queen. I want to feel this way every day.

Mitch: I need to see you. "Funtyme 911."

Karah: Our future may not be certain. But this feeling—I must have it. ☺

Mitch: You are my queen. "Funtyme 911."

Mitch: I ADORE YOU! "Funtyme 911."

Karah: That makes my heart skip a beat and puts a big smile on my face. We will meet soon. I must get myself under control. Right now, my emotions are making me think too far ahead. I think I'd say yes to anything you ask.

Mitch: Are you scared to fall in love with a younger man? "Funtyme 911."

Karah: My husband was younger. So, no, if ... you will take care of my heart. Will you? Will YOU take care of my heart? I'm writing today, and I need to focus. ☹

Mitch: OK, I may not be able to respond right away, but text me EVERY TIME you feel me. "Funtyme 911."

Karah: I will, sweetie, and don't forget about me.

Mitch: Never. TTYL. "Funtyme 911."

Karah: Wait—tell me you will take care of me.

Mitch: Boo, I will treat you like a rose and nurture you gently every day ... "Funtyme 911."

Karah: Please rescue me ... I want to be in your arms, not working on this book.

Mitch: I feel you, boo. Things may be worse once we finally get together. We will never want to be apart! "Funtyme 911."

Karah: The thought of that gave me butterflies! Normally, I'm Zena, the Warrior Princess, but my powers are questionable when it comes to you.

Mitch: Well, I'm Mitch, aka Funtyme 911, but don't let the tagline fool you. I adore you, and you have the power of love over me. "Funtyme 911."

Mitch: Hey, I'm a good guy, boo. I will not hurt you. Just love you. Spend quality time with you. Travel with you. Give me a chance. "Funtyme 911."

Karah: Ohhh … you make me feel so special. I will make you a very happy man.

Mitch: Are you sure? I've been praying for a good woman. "Funtyme 911."

Karah: I would love to be the one. I am serious, just very protective of my heart. I want to fall in love with no limits. If I can't, then what's the use?

Mitch: Girl, I got you! Let's go for it. "Funtyme 911."

Mitch: The sky is the limit for my love. "Funtyme 911."

Mitch: But will your family have an issue with you dating a younger man?

Karah: You're not that much younger. But will your family have a problem?

        I know if my son came home with some chick my age, I would be like that mother in *How Stella Got Her Groove Back*. I'd take her in the back room and …

Mitch: I'm good on that end, boo. My family will love you. "Funtyme 911."

Karah: Me too … I think. LOL. Seriously, I always must put my foot down with my clan. What about young chicks, posting up on my man?

Mitch: No worries, boo; that's why we need to meet soon. We have so much to talk about in person, and we can't move forward until we both have a good understanding. "Funtyme 911."

Mitch: I will not make trouble, but I will not let anyone stop us if we're on the same page. "Funtyme 911."

Karah: No worries; my children are all grown and on their own.

Karah: Only my baby boy lives here with me … he's a film maker, trying to find his niche in life.

Karah: Mitch. Honey … are you there?

Mitch: Sorry, boo, I was taking a shower, getting ready for a meeting. Club members planning a leadership dinner, so let me finish getting dressed and then I'll reply. "Funtyme 911."

Karah: OK.

Mitch: That's great—filmmaker and writer in the same house? Wow. "Funtyme 911."

Mitch: Hey, boo, I hope we can meet soon. We're getting kind of deep not to have even met. Let's look into each other's eyes and lay it all on the table. "Funtyme 911"

Mitch: There's a lot more to me than you know. I have lots of goals, and I need my girl by my side. We really need to talk face-to-face. "Funtyme 911."

Karah: I do not doubt you, sweetie. I like you and feel good about you.

Mitch: Girl, I'm trying to be your man, and you are making it too hard. Why? Just think about that question, and let's talk about it later. Got to make this meeting. Call you later. "Funtyme 911."

Karah: Okay. Be safe. Muah!

Things started to get testy between Mitch and me, even though we had not met in person. He sensed my reluctance to meet him. Our emotions were taking our texting in the opposite direction. When he called later, he started the conversation where we'd left off when we were texting.

"Hey, let's discuss my last question. I just don't get you. I'm starting to think you have a hidden agenda."

"No, I don't. I just don't trust so quickly."

"Boo, we have to meet before trust will come. I'm trying to make you my woman."

"I choose men," I told him. "Men don't choose me. But if I have chosen you as my man, there is nothing I can't do or wouldn't do to please you—nothing. But don't rush me. Please. Why didn't you text me back last night? I saw you online. I hope you did not ignore me, your boo, for some bullshit."

"Oh, my goodness, Karah. Not everyone is on there for dates. I do a lot of my business on that site."

"It doesn't matter If you see me anywhere, you will acknowledge me. I don't care who you talk to or what you talk about."

"I didn't see you, girl, and you need to stay off that site. What are you looking for when you haven't even met me?"

"We are both grown, and I am not insecure. I only want the man God has for me. Everyone else is just entertainment."

"Entertainment? Well, I'm not that guy!"

"Fine, but you were inconsiderate of me … and that's not acceptable."

"Karah, I have a business, and I buy and sell stuff all the time, online and offline. I have time for you, but I have to make my money as well. I will be true to you."

"You are missing the point. In a new relationship it is important to understand each other. I understand your position, your work … your business. No problem. Do your thang. I wish you much success, whether we come together or not.

And if you're too busy for me, I can understand that, but if I get the feeling you're ignoring me, or you just don't give a damn, you can't justify it. No excuses!"

"Oh my God, oh my God, oh my God!"

"Oh my God is right … I'm going to sleep. I will no longer bother you."

"Girl you are tripping, but fine, good night."

It wasn't long after we hung up that he sent me a text:

Mitch: Hey, boo, I'm seriously thinking maybe I'm not the man for you. We are fussing already, and I haven't even met you. So I'll just pull back and be your homeboy. if you accept. "Funtyme 911."

Mitch: I'm a great guy. Someday the right girl will see that! "Funtyme 911."

Karah: I'm a great girl, and the man for me will be supportive. I'm on a mission. I write books, market them, and am trying to find a movie deal. I can't be upset or distracted.

Mitch: I've tried to see you, call you, and love you like I know how, but you will not give us a chance. You're so focused on the negative. "Funtyme 911."

Karah: I just don't like being squeezed into your busy schedule. If you don't have time to call or text, how are you going to have time to date or anything else?

This relationship was unbelievable. My emotions were all over the place, and I needed to just let go, but every time I tried, Mitch would pull me right back in. We were constantly up and down. I think we were both strong people and were each accustomed to being in control. Now we each faced the possibility of losing that control, and we were fighting hard to keep it.

There was a trust issue. One day I saw him as a sweet, loving man, and then other days I saw him as an internet predator who had been playing these games for years. The only way I could have any control over that was if he fell in love with me.

Love will make you change. So I felt that even if he had bad intentions, he wouldn't follow through if his heart was involved. The sad part was that if we didn't meet, we wouldn't even know if it was worth the fight.

Still, day after day, week after week, we kept this wild ride on full throttle.

Mitch	It's time to decide. Not once have you asked to see me. Phone/texting is all good, but we need in-person contact! This is ridiculous. "Funtyme 911."
Karah	Really, well we will meet in due time. It's only been a couple of months, and I told you I needed time.
Karah	You have me. I like you, I want you, I need you, but I don't think you feel the same. You seem to think … you have it all, and I should be honored and *jump* at the opportunity to be your boo.
Karah	Well, I feel the opposite. I am a queen. You should be honored. One day you will see that!
Karah	And no, you can't be my freaking … homeboy! My heart doesn't ache for my homeboys. You are tripping.
Mitch	OMG … we both should be jumping at each other, boo. "Funtyme 911."
Karah	Yesterday you wanted to take me to the moon; today to the hood—homeboy, really? You got me confused. Look at my pictures. Do I look like I need a homeboy?
Mitch	You are a mess! OMG. "Funtyme 911."
Mitch	I'd rather see your lips, so I can kiss them. "Funtyme 911."
Karah	I am tired of arguing with you.
Karah	Then a kiss it shall be. MUAH … bye.
Mitch	Well, I am not begging. Muah, bye. "Funtyme 911."
Mitch	Good morning. Can we meet on Sunday? "Funtyme 911."
Karah	Sure, I can't wait. Anytime … any place.
Mitch	Are you going to be my girl! "Funtyme 911."
Karah	I think so. We have to stop fighting against it.
Karah	I feel you deep in my heart.

Mitch	I think so too. Just stop tripping out on me. "Funtyme 911."
Karah	Don't call my concerns "tripping." I want you. You want me. Let's meet first before we commit to anything more.
Mitch	Let's take care of each other. We must stop bailing out every time we have a misunderstanding. "Funtyme 911."
Karah	Friends, lovers, partners for life—we are not sure. But always remember that we are each precious to God. He brought us together for a reason. Given time, we will find out why.
Mitch	I know I want you! I don't need a sign from above to know that. "Funtyme 911."
Karah	LOL. Whatever. I am your friend. We did meet online. I picked you out of hundreds.
Mitch	So why do you get mad when I ask you to send photos? "Funtyme 911."
Karah	That was then …
Karah	And like I said, I cannot take good body shots with this camera.
Mitch	OMG, here we go again "Funtyme 911."
Karah	I'm just not comfortable with that.
Mitch	I just want a photo of you! "Funtyme 911."
Karah	Will do.
Karah	Full body.
Mitch	Nude … xxx. "Funtyme 911."
Karah	So you got me in here ….. sweating … posing … timer going off too soon … or not at all … when all you wanted was to see my ass.
Karah	Damn.
Karah	I thought you wanted to see how fat I am.
Mitch	I just want to see you, boo. "Funtyme 911."

Karah   Oh, like looking at my naked body is going to give you a complete picture of me. Ass!

Mitch   Don't put words in my mouth, please. "Funtyme 911."

Karah   I won't. Enough said. That just made you look like everyone else. Doggish!

Karah   I will not be sending any more communications.

Mitch   I know who I am, and God knows. If you think otherwise, that's on you. Be blessed, home girl … "Funtyme 911."

Karah   Ass!

Karah   I am woman enough to say I'm sorry when I'm wrong and strong enough to walk away when I need to. It's almost Thanksgiving, and I must give thanks to God for this experience. I wish only the best for you … again. I'm sorry for any hurtful words I spoke and sorry I can't be exactly what you need. I had only good intentions

Mitch   Be blessed! Friends—Home Girl 4 Life! "Funtyme 911."

Karah   Whatever!

Mitch   You're stressing me out. I didn't want you to send me a nude photo. I was just kidding. You blow things out of proportion. "Funtyme 911."

Mitch   All I asked was to meet you, and you changed the subject every time, so maybe you already have a man. I don't know "Funtyme 911."

Karah   I said I'm sorry. Don't mean to stress you or me. That's why I say stop.

Mitch   I can't; you stole my heart! "Funtyme 911."

Karah   The fact that you can hurt me is not good. The fact that you don't realize it makes it worse.

Mitch   See, that's what I mean! You think it's all about you. Men hurt too! It hurts when you say I'm mean when I know I'm not. "Funtyme 911."

Karah   No, I never said you were mean, but I do feel that you cannot relate to my feelings. I am not unreasonable or irrational. Things that concern me should concern you.

Karah   But it's Okay. Stupid me. I take full responsibility for my behavior.

Mitch   Likewise, but all I'm hearing you speak is me, me, me. How about us? "Funtyme 911."

Karah   We just can't get it together.

Mitch   OMG ... well, maybe all those others trying to get at you will be better at what you say I'm not. "Funtyme 911."

Mitch   Home girl may work better since I don't meet your standards! "Funtyme 911."

Karah   Oh really.

Karah   I will not be your freaking ... home girl. All or nothing. I do understand that some things just don't work out.

Karah   I will never regret knowing you ... feeling you so deeply. I can only look forward to the day when it will all come together, and we both have our TRUE mates.

Karah   I am sorry for any stress I caused you.

Mitch   I'm good, boo. "Funtyme 911."

Karah   Okay ... It's Thanksgiving time, and I'm the cook.

Mitch   You know you're in love with me, so stop playing! "Funtyme 911."

Karah   That may be true. My foolish heart is weak, but my mind and prayers are strong. And they will see me through.

Karah   I got to go cook. Can't be dragging around like a lovesick puppy.

Mitch   So if I say I'm in love with you, what would you say? "Funtyme 911."

Karah   I'd say we both have a problem because we can't get along.

Karah	Love is beautiful. The fact that we can't share it and express it together is sad.
Karah	God has granted us love, but all this other crap is creating confusion and is not of God.
Mitch	IKR … if you don't want to be my boo just say so. "Funtyme 911."
Karah	Now you're stressing me out.
Mitch	OMG … well we don't need that, do we? "Funtyme 911."
Karah	And it doesn't seem to matter to you one way or the other.
Mitch	LOL. You are my boo-boo anyway. "Funtyme 911."
Karah	You think it's a game.
Mitch	No, I need you. Do you need me? "Funtyme 911."
Karah	Yes.
Karah	But I'm not willing to give up my peace of mind.
Karah	I want and need to be loved unconditionally.
Karah	I don't think you are ready for me.
Mitch	OMG. OMG. OMG. OMG. Good night. "Funtyme 911."
Karah	Good night.
Karah	I took this for you earlier, before we broke up. Remember I am 57. [I sent him a full photo.]
Karah	I'm not ashamed of my body.
Mitch	Wow, thank you. That's all I wanted. Miss you dearly! "Funtyme 911."
Mitch	Morning, boo. "Funtyme 911."
Karah	Good morning, Mitch.
Karah	I still like you, but I think I better just wish you the best and move on. No regrets.
Mitch	If you really like me, let's work things out! "Funtyme 911."
Mitch	You are all over my mind! "Funtyme 911."

Mitch	I really like you a lot. I'm so broken-hearted. I was sad all night. "Funtyme 911."
Karah	We each have so much going on. We can't be stressing each other.
Karah	It interferes with my writing.
Karah	I miss my friend. Wish we could find that peaceful, supportive, loving place with each other.
Karah	You still stay on my mind either way. So sad. Let's just pray about it.
Mitch	I pray every day, but I'll pray extra hard 'cause I really want you in my life. "Funtyme 911."
Karah	I think we're both scared
Mitch	IKR. "Funtyme 911."
Mitch	I just need to hold you.
Mitch	Maybe that will bond us together.
Karah	Our feelings for each other are real.
Karah	We can't deny that.
Karah	But we are disconnected right now.
Karah	It's been a long time since you said you adore me.
Karah	Tell me you still adore me.
Mitch	Girl, you know I adore you with your sexy self! "Funtyme 911."
Karah	Then don't let me go.
Mitch	I'm trying to hold on to you. Men are not supposed to be scared, but my heart is gentle. "Funtyme 911."
Karah	I'm just not sure anymore.
Mitch	I'm not sure how much longer I can go without seeing you! "Funtyme 911."
Mitch	I've never text-felt this way about someone so soon before! "Funtyme 911."

Mitch	I'm open to do anything to make it better for us! "Funtyme 911."
Mitch	I adore you to the fullest. "Funtyme 911."
Karah	Let me think about everything. Let's talk later.
Mitch	Do you miss me yet! Call me. "Funtyme 911"

When Mitch called later, I told him I missed him. "In fact, I've been missing you all day."

"I want to give you a big wet kiss!" he responded.

"Our relationship is amusing to say the least. What are we going to do? Who are you? What are you trying to do—steal my heart?"

"Girl ... I'm already in love with you! I'll be the man of your dreams, your knight who come to make you my queen!

"All that, and we've never met."

"Yes, people meet this way all the time. I know what you look like, what you sound like, and many things about you. Unless it's all a lie—now that's when I start to panic."

"Don't panic, sweetie. I am who I say I am. No deception, no lies."

"Same here, so let's just calm down. We will meet in person soon."

"Okay, sweetie, I agree. I've got to start cooking. Text me later."

"Sure," he said. Instead, he called me, screaming, "OMG! Are you enjoying being online?"

"What? I'm not online. I'm cooking. I was there earlier. I might still be logged on. If so, I'll log off. Do your thang."

"Huh ... LMAO."

"It's Thanksgiving," I told him. "No time for this foolishness. I'm cooking. Bye."
Later, I sent him another text.

Karah	I'm done in the kitchen. My head is all stuffed up. Feeling no love from you. Going to bed. Good night.
Mitch	Happy Thanksgiving! Be blessed. "Funtyme 911."
Karah	I am blocking you. You be blessed.
Mitch	Cool! "Funtyme 911."
Karah	I figured the dating site that brought us together would become a problem. I'm blocking you. Delete my number … now. I'm deleting yours.
Mitch	I can't do this anymore either. UR too much to deal with. Good luck … no reply needed. "Funtyme 911."
Karah	You are not in charge of me. I will reply if I want to. Block me … don't read … whatever.
Karah	Please delete my photos.
Mitch	No! They are mine now. "Funtyme 911."
Karah	Delete my pics like I asked, please.
Mitch	I already did. "Funtyme 911."
Karah	Thanks. Now I will delete all your info. No regrets.
Mitch	Cool. It's all good, boo "Funtyme 911."
Mitch	Sweet dreams. "Funtyme 911."
Mitch	Good morning! "Funtyme 911."
Karah	OMG!
Karah	I was just praying about us.
Karah	I miss my friend.
Karah	How are you?
Mitch	We need to talk. I didn't sleep all night. "Funtyme 911."
Karah	Me either. I am in trouble here, and I need my friend.
Mitch	What kind of trouble? I'm here for you. "Funtyme 911."
Karah	Thank you. My heart aches … for you.
Karah	I need some help understanding.

Mitch   I'm in love with you. "Funtyme 911."

Karah   How?

Karah   Why?

Karah   What am I supposed to do?

Mitch   It's okay for us to tell our real feeling or show them. What makes it seem weird is that we've never actually met. I knew this could become a problem. "Funtyme 911."

Mitch   Let me ask you—do you care about me? I mean, does it matter if I stay in your life or go? "Funtyme 911."

Karah   Yes, and I don't want to push you away.

Karah   But I am so afraid.

Mitch   Afraid of what? "Funtyme 911."

Karah   Losing control.

Karah   Who are you? This man I expect to take care of my heart.

Karah   Are you to be my friend? Or my soul mate?

Mitch   Soon, there will be no difference. "Funtyme 911."

Karah   I don't want to confuse our relationship.

Karah   I know this frustrates you, but you must understand my position.

Karah   Understanding will keep us strong.

Mitch   I promise to be honest and true with you about everything. "Funtyme 911."

Mitch   I want you to do the same. "Funtyme 911."

Mitch   I really like you a lot, and I want to keep you in my life. "Funtyme 911."

Mitch   We really must get to know each other. "Funtyme 911."

Mitch   I am praying about it, asking God to put our relationship on solid ground. "Funtyme 911."

Mitch   I am his child, and I have his work to do. "Funtyme 911."

Mitch	I cannot be side-tracked unless it's true. Friendship or not. "Funtyme 911."
Mitch	Why are you losing control? Do you really wish for me to stay away? "Funtyme 911."
Karah	No.
Karah	Don't go.
Karah	Please stay.
Karah	I need you.
Mitch	Well, I try to love you and take care of you, but I think you get scared and run away because you might adore and love me as well! "Funtyme 911."
Karah	I truly believe that I am in love with you.
Mitch	I'm always true and honest! I'm a great guy and God knows that, and he sits high and looks low and keeps blessing me! "Funtyme 911."
Karah	But I told you my fears from the start.
Karah	You told me … you got me. Then you got frustrated and wanted me to go.
Mitch	We can't get to know each other if we never see each other. I need you to know that for some reason, my heart tells me you can't meet because you have someone! "Funtyme 911."
Karah	Oh no, I have no other man in my life. I wouldn't be doing this if I did.
Karah	I don't cheat.
Mitch	I don't either, love is only as good as we make it. "Funtyme 911."
Mitch	Girl, I need you! We need each other. "Funtyme 911."
Karah	Well, please forget about there being someone else in my life.
Karah	My life is open for you, sweetie. Trust me.
Mitch	I'm trying to, but you need to trust me as well. "Funtyme 911."

Karah	Okay, but I must say what's on my mind, and that's when things get rough between us.
Karah	We are both strong and going to stand our ground. I understand that, but we need to find a neutral place.
Karah	I want to let my guard down; my shoulders hurt from being on the defensive. But that's my way. I've been that way all my life. Not because I've been hurt but because I don't want to be.
Mitch	I will not hurt you! I just want to love you. "Funtyme 911."
Karah	Listen, we are both strong believers, beautiful children of God. Can we come together as one?
Mitch	Yes, I know we can. "Funtyme 911."
Karah	If we want to come together as one, let's just do it. Let's just step out on our faith and give it a try.
Karah	We are both single; there is no reason why we can't.
Mitch	That would be so nice. "Funtyme 911."
Karah	Okay, Mitch, my guard is coming down.
Karah	I promise to be extra careful not to let my insecurities create unnecessary problems for us.
Karah	I want to be your boo.
Karah	I want you to adore me.
Mitch	And I want to take care of you and keep a smile on your face. "Funtyme 911."
Karah	We can meet anytime … anywhere.
Karah	Don't get upset when I say this.
Karah	Never mind. LOL.
Mitch	When you're free, let's meet, boo. It's time. "Funtyme 911."
Mitch	I do adore you! "Funtyme 911."
Karah	I adore you, sweetie.
Mitch	Do you love me? "Funtyme 911."

Karah	Yes, I love you!
Mitch	I love you. "Funtyme 911."
Mitch	Does that make you happy? "Funtyme 911."
Karah	Yes! Muah … Muah … Muah.
Mitch	OK, time to have sweet dreams now. Good night, love. "Funtyme 911."
Karah	Nite-nite, sweetie.
Mitch	Good morning. I love and adore you! "Funtyme 911."
Karah	Now that put a sweet, sexy smile on my face. Good morning!
Mitch	If you text me, and I don't text right back, it's because I'm busy washing my car. Don't get upset. "Funtyme 911."
Karah	Of course not. I have a new attitude. [I sent him a photo, one in which I was smiling.]
Karah	Thanks for this bright morning smile. [Then I sent another that showed I was doing a dance.]
Karah	Thinking of you. Dancing my ass off!
Karah	Must start writing at ten. Love you. Have a blessed day!
Mitch	You too, and thanks for the photos. Muah! "Funtyme 911."
Karah	Muah.
Mitch	Kissing you back, love! "Funtyme 911."
Karah	Ms. Karah got her swag back.
Karah	And she is flaunting it today.
Mitch	You never lost it, love! "Funtyme 911."
Mitch	I can't stand being away from you any longer! "Funtyme 911."
Karah	We will fix it soon. Just keep me close to your heart for now.
Mitch	You do the same, love. I still adore you. "Funtyme 911."
Karah	Every time you say that, my heart skips a beat, and something grips my sweet spot.
Karah	I promise when you say it in my ear, I am going to …

Mitch	I believe we truly are a match. Many things attracted me to you. "Funtyme 911."
Mitch	I am very comfortable with where we are—friends who love and adore each other. "Funtyme 911."
Karah	You are the only man to captivate me in a very long time.
Karah	And I believe in the power of the Father.
Karah	I am a realist. I only want the man chosen for me by God.
Mitch	Don't be afraid. I will always keep it real. "Funtyme 911."
Karah	Today, let's just celebrate this love we feel and thank God for bringing us together.
Mitch	Yes, I am your king, and you're my queen for life, so let me love and adore you as we worship God together! "Funtyme 911."
Karah	That is so sweet.
Karah	Fairy tales do come true.
Mitch	Hell, yes, they do. Real love is waiting for us. You just wait and see! "Funtyme 911."
Karah	People often ask why I'm single; only God knows why. But I feel like I'm supposed to have a mate … but only in God's time.
Mitch	This is God's time. "Funtyme 911."
Karah	Most men I've dated would come back to me if they could. Still, it didn't work.
Karah	That wasn't in God's plans. That's the way I see it.
Mitch	Well, out of all the people on the site, we were attracted to each other. What about that? "Funtyme 911."
Karah	That is special, no matter how you slice it.
Mitch	I want to love you, hold you, rub your feet, hold your hands. "Funtyme 911."
Karah	OMG.
Karah	And I would let you. LOL.

Mitch	Hey, love, what are you doing? "Funtyme 911."
Karah	Hey, baby.
Karah	I'm writing. I'm in that zone, and it feels good.
Mitch	Cool. "Funtyme 911."
Karah	Oh no, I have time for you, sweetie.
Karah	You are my inspiration.
Mitch	I love my baby. We have so much to talk over. "Funtyme 911."
Karah	Such as?
Mitch	Just sharing … thoughts … ideas … goals. "Funtyme 911."
Karah	I can't wait.
Karah	Mitch, I need to say something.
Mitch	Go ahead. "Funtyme 911."
Karah	Mitch, I will never compete with anything or anyone for your time. If I'm your queen, you will make sure I don't have to.
Mitch	OMG, you wouldn't have to, baby! "Funtyme 911."
Karah	I love you, sweetie.
Mitch	I adore you! "Funtyme 911."
Karah	I love this feeling.
Karah	You make me very relaxed.
Karah	Sexy.
Karah	Sweet.
Karah	If you touched me now, I'd explode.
Mitch	I look forward to taking you for a ride, mentally and physically. "Funtyme 911."
Karah	I want you.
Karah	I need you.
Karah	Say … my name. Say Karah. Say it. Close your eyes and say it.

Mitch	Girl, stop, I wish I was holding you right now! "Funtyme 911."
Mitch	Good morning, my queen! "Funtyme 911."
Karah	Good morning, sweetie.
Karah	I slept with this phone again.
Mitch	That's great. I'm up early for work, thinking about my goddess, my queen, my pearl! "Funtyme 911."
Karah	I am starting to feel comfortable as all three.
Mitch	I need for you to hold me. "Funtyme 911."
Karah	I'm ready.
Karah	I'm smiling.
Karah	I think we are alike in many ways.
Mitch	That's great. I love your smile, and I promise to keep you smiling. "Funtyme 911."
Karah	So maybe this is a good time for me to express my feelings. Call me.
Mitch	Sure. "Funtyme 911."

He called within seconds, and I answered immediately.

"Hey ba, my body is on fire all over. I mean, really; it is unbelievable."

"Maybe if I rub your body in baby oil all over, you will cool down a little. Would you like that?"

"Boo, if you touch me, I will explode."

"My love for you is very real—different. It's so strong it grabs my heart, soul, and mind very deeply and will not let go. I will never want to leave you."

"Then what will you do with me?"

"I'm gonna do everything with you. Where would you like me to start? Your choice. What would you like? Be real!"

"Take me to the highest level of love," I said, "and don't let me go. You will experience that same kind of love. Know what you want from the start. If you love me, make me know it. Don't hold back; don't play games. I will do the same. We are both strong people, but let's give and receive love freely."

"I don't play games either," he said. "If I get a bad taste in my mouth, it's a wrap! Let's keep our love alive and always burning."

"Strength should not be required when it comes to my man. I plan to let my guard down and free-fall into love with no limits. I am not afraid. I believe our love is meant to be, and I will embrace it. I have very high ethical and moral standards, and I pride myself on being the total woman. I want you to do the same. I want to make you happy and in love with me. True love will prevail."

"There is no turning back now. I am in love with you. So we will go forward! I've got to go, love. Talk to you soon."

"OMG … this is truly happening! Okay, sweetie. Muah. Hey, there is still one big obstacle—chemistry."

"That will not be a problem," Mitch insisted. "Let's just stay in the love zone, love. Don't focus on anything negative."

His response made me laugh with delight. "Good answer, ba. The chemistry between us will be no problem."

"Yep, all that BS is going to stop. I adore you to the fullest!"

Mitch	Hey love! "Funtyme 911."
Karah	Good morning, sweet man of mine.
Karah	I'm missing you so much. [He sent a photo.]
Mitch	Enjoying my day at work. "Funtyme 911."
Karah	Thank you, sweetie. I needed that.
Karah	OMG—sexy.

Mitch	I try, Boo! "Funtyme 911."
Karah	Tell me you want me. Tell me you adore me. Tell me something because I am tripping bad.
Mitch	Why are you tripping? I adore you. I need you. I'm feeling you. I'm super hot for you. You are my world. You're my queen. "Funtyme 911."
Karah	Aw. I'm better now.
Karah	I'm fine, really.
Karah	I looked at you and thought, Damn, he looks better and better every time.
Mitch	Thank you, boo. "Funtyme 911."
Mitch	Girl, when … when will we meet? "Funtyme 911."
Karah	Whenever you say.
Mitch	I was ready day one. Still waiting on you, boo. "Funtyme 911."
Karah	I think it's time, but this is a bad weekend.
Karah	I'm writing this weekend, and I can't stop.
Karah	A few more chapters; then I'll send it to the editors.
Karah	After that, I'm free.
Mitch	I just have to wait until you get ready. "Funtyme 911."
Karah	We will see each other soon … I promise.
Mitch	Sounds great. Can't wait. "Funtyme 911."
Karah	I got to go write. TTYL.
Mitch	Okay, baby, have a good night. "Funtyme 911."
Karah	You too, sweetie.

When it came to the entire internet-dating adventure, I was staggered by my own behavior. I went from being afraid of some nut cutting my head off to saying *I love you* and committing myself to a man I'd never even met. I could see how women or men would travel across the country to meet a stranger. It had gotten to the point where

I didn't see Mitch as a stranger. He was my friend. He didn't seem to have a hidden agenda. He had never asked me for money or suggested anything sinister. He seemed to be honest and as afraid of me as I was of him. At this point, however, I was getting terrified again. We had allowed this love to grow through written communication and phone calls. Now we had to come face-to-face, and all I could think of was, *What if we don't like each other?* Sure, we'd exchanged pictures, sometimes on the spot, so I didn't expect there to be any major disappointments there. But there were so many other character traits and personality issues that could be a complete turn-off. This is what my loneliness and curiosity had led to, and now my heart was involved. There was no turning back. I had to meet Mitch face-to-face.

Karah	Mitch?
Mitch	Yes, boo. "Funtyme 911."
Karah	I have some concerns.
Mitch	Go on. "Funtyme 911."
Karah	I don't want to disappoint you.
Karah	I want everything to be just right.
Karah	Vibes … appearance … chemistry.
Mitch	Girl, stop; just meet me face-to-face. That's all I ask. "Funtyme 911."
Karah	Okay, sweetie, and if we get those vibes, we can sleep in each other's arms.
Mitch	Are you sure staying the night in each other's arms will not be too much? "Funtyme 911."
Karah	No. I think we need to comfort each other. Hold each other.
Karah	We have been on an emotional roller coaster for a few weeks.
Mitch	That's all behind us now. "Funtyme 911."
Mitch	Let's just keep it real. "Funtyme 911."

Mitch	I look forward to spending the night with you. And absolutely no sex on our first encounter. "Funtyme 911."
Karah	Even if I beg?
Karah	I mean, really beg?
Karah	LOL.
Mitch	Holding you is good for me. "Funtyme 911."
Mitch	Sex brings drama at times. "Funtyme 911."
Karah	Really? Please explain.
Mitch	Sometimes people get out of control over sex. "Funtyme 911."
Karah	Very interesting.
Karah	Well, let me say this—I have never been out of control.
Karah	Especially over sex.
Karah	Don't try to make me suffer for someone else's issues.
Karah	If I want it, you will give it to me!
Karah	With pleasure.
Mitch	Okay, boo-boo, let's not make this an issue. "Funtyme 911."
Mitch	And boo, everything that you have felt, done, or handled in the past, forget about that. Why? Because I'm a rare breed, and it's going to be out of this world. So hold on tight. "Funtyme 911."
Karah	I am too old with too many goals to be losing control.
Karah	Not now. I don't need a magic show.
Karah	Besides, I am a grown-ass woman. Lovemaking, no matter how incredible, will not control me.
Karah	Hearing you say "I adore you" is much more effective. Trust me.
Karah	If—and only if—God has chosen you to be my king could your skills blow me away, and I will welcome that.
Karah	If your skills are worldly—practiced and perfected, with other women—they will have no permanent effect on me.

Mitch	In due time, we will see. "Funtyme 911."
Mitch	My skills are from years ago. I'm good at what I do. "Funtyme 911."
Mitch	I can talk to you on the phone and make you blow a gasket. "Funtyme 911."
Karah	LOL. I'm scared of you.
Mitch	Don't be, because afterward, I'll stay on the phone and listen to you sleep. "Funtyme 911."
Karah	Oh no, I don't want to be strung out.
Mitch	You are my sweet baby. I love you. Good night. "Funtyme 911."
Karah	Wow ... I don't think I can sleep after hearing that, but I'll try. TTYL.
Karah	GM, your texts from last night are amusing. Too bad I was half asleep.
Mitch	Great morning, love. "Funtyme 911."
Karah	Is it really possible that your sex will drive me crazy?
Mitch	It can happen, but I'll take it nice and slow with you! "Funtyme 911."
Karah	God didn't bring you into my life so I can go crazy.
Karah	That would be Satan. And in the name of Jesus, I have some powers over him.
Mitch	Cool, but I must make it great, or why do it. "Funtyme 911."
Karah	If God placed me in your life, be advised—handle with care.
Mitch	I will. Real talk. I'm only ready when you are, not before then! "Funtyme 911."
Karah	Okay, sweetie. At least you're not sex-crazy.
Mitch	No, I'm not! "Funtyme 911."
Karah	Good. That will go a long way with me.

Mitch	I know that's right, coming from the one who's gone without for two freaking years. "Funtyme 911."
Karah	LOL. By God's grace, I am very disciplined. Please tell me you adore me.
Mitch	I adore you, baby. "Funtyme 911."
Mitch	Muah. "Funtyme 911."
Mitch	I can kiss on you all day and night! "Funtyme 911."
Karah	Please do; you make me feel sexy.
Mitch	You are sexy and fine. I need you to know that too! "Funtyme 911."
Mitch	All day, every day? "Funtyme 911."
Karah	Oh yes, I do, but its enhanced when I know my king adores me.
Karah	Muah.
Mitch	Kiss, kiss. "Funtyme 911."
Karah	I miss you. ☹
Mitch	I adore you, boo. "Funtyme 911."
Karah	☺
Karah	I'm so tired.
Karah	Long day. I need to sleep.
Karah	So I took something that will have me out like a light shortly.
Mitch	I love U, girl! "Funtyme 911."
Mitch	Get some sleep. "Funtyme 911."
Karah	Hey sexy, I still miss you.
Mitch	And I still adore you. "Funtyme 911."
Mitch	Did you have a restful night? "Funtyme 911."
Karah	Yes, I sure did.
Mitch	I'm glad, love. "Funtyme 911."

Karah	Can you take me to the moon and back with this love of yours?
Mitch	I plan to! "Funtyme 911."
Mitch	Are you going to always be my boo? "Funtyme 911."
Karah	Yes, unless …
Karah	1. I find you to be a crazy psycho.
Karah	2. You're married or have another who thinks she's your boo.
Mitch	If I am not who I say I am, I expect you to back up. I will do the same. "Funtyme 911."
Karah	No, I don't think you read that right. If you're a liar, I will not back up. I am out—plain and simple.
Mitch	You need to meet me, and look in my eyes. I don't lie. "Funtyme 911."
Karah	Picture sent.
Mitch	Wow, thanks, girl. I love your sexy-ass smile. "Funtyme 911."
Karah	Then keep me smiling, sweetie.
Karah	I miss you. ☹
Mitch	Hey, boo, I'm so sorry I had to go out of town for a few days. Family drama, and I just didn't get to call. "Funtyme 911."
Karah	Really? I'm sorry to hear that.
Mitch	Yeah, it was very bad! I'll tell you about it over the phone later. "Funtyme 911."
Karah	That's not necessary, unless you need to talk.
Mitch	No, but I do need to hear your voice. "Funtyme 911."
Karah	Call me when you can.

It was late the next day before I heard from Mitch. He apologized for the delay and explained that at this time of year, it was hard for him to text or talk. He would be working twelve-hour days and would be exhausted. He also explained that his oldest child lived in Texas and had gotten into some trouble. He'd had to go down immediately and deal with the situation. All I could say was that I understood because when it came to work or children, nothing was more important.

The next few weeks went by so fast. I was focused on getting my manuscript to the editors, and Mitch continued to work twelve-hour shifts. We still sent affectionate texts throughout the day or had a few short phone calls. We were both busy and both understood.

Mitch	Merry Christmas, sweet lady. I wish I could give you diamonds and pearls and make your heart smile. "Funtyme 911."
Karah	Thank you, dear, and merry Christmas to you. Are you being a good Santa?
Mitch	Yes, Santa and Santa's helpers. I been wrapping gifts and putting stuff together like a madman—plus giving out money like an ATM. "Funtyme 911."
Mitch	But our time is coming, and when we meet, I will give you your Christmas present. Do you miss me? "Funtyme 911."
Karah	More than you can imagine, but I didn't get you a gift.
Mitch	Please, don't even think about it. You are my baby doll. I just want to hold you! I can't wait! "Funtyme 911."
Karah	I love you, sweetie.
Mitch	Love you, too. Got to go—duty calls. "Funtyme 911."
Karah	Okay, sweetie. Don't forget about me.
Mitch	Never! We'll talk later. Muah. "Funtyme 911."
Karah	I miss you.
Karah	Damn, Mitch! I haven't heard from you in a week.
Mitch	Hey, love … I don't want to frustrate you. I'm sorry—just working, boo. Between my job, my church, and my family, I'm running all over the place. "Funtyme 911."
Karah	I've been busy too, but I still text you, and you can't even reply.

	I was worried about you, and it's not like someone would let me know if something happened to you. Nobody even knows I exist.
Mitch	My sisters do, and if anything happened, they know how to reach you. Does any of your family know I exist? "Funtyme 911."
Karah	No, but they will.
Mitch	Long days at work—that takes up most of my time—but I got to make this money, boo. I'm behind from the holidays. "Funtyme 911."
Karah	I understand that, but my goodness. This is what I'm afraid of. You will not have time for me. And I'll end up being just a piece of ...
Mitch	Look, I'm not looking for a booty call from you. I don't play that way. "Funtyme 911."
Mitch	I love you and miss you a lot! I'm working—that's all. "Funtyme 911."
Karah	You're my sweet baby. I just miss you.
Mitch	I know, boo; me too. "Funtyme 911."
Mitch	Good morning, sexy. I fell asleep last night. I'm sorry. "Funtyme 911."
Karah	I figured that; no need to apologize.
Mitch	Things are settling down, now that tree is back in the attic. LOL. Now we can get back to us. "Funtyme 911."
Karah	Happy ... smiling.
Mitch	Great—me too. "Funtyme 911."
Karah	Make me yours, Mitch.
	I love you.
Mitch	I adore you. "Funtyme 911."
Karah	That makes me very happy.
	Love you ... be safe.

Mitch	Sending you a video. "Funtyme 911."
Karah	Wow, that was beautiful. I love Minnie Riperton.
	If those lyrics represent what you feel, I have found my soul mate.
Mitch	"Loving You" says exactly what I'm feeling. "Funtyme 911."
Karah	I'm going to scream!
Mitch	Go ahead, love. It's all about you! "Funtyme 911."
Karah	No, it's all about us. I want you to feel like screaming too. We each should be excited.
Mitch	I am a good person—good to you and good for you. "Funtyme 911."
Karah	Thank God!
	I already feel much more complete.
Mitch	Good. I got you, girl. "Funtyme 911."
Karah	And God's blessings will allow us to grow together as one.
Mitch	We will; I'm sure of that. "Funtyme 911."
Karah	I am in the clouds.
	This is such a rare and welcome emotional high for me.
Mitch	K. I'll be home in an hour. I'll call you. I want to hear your sweet voice. "Funtyme 911."
Karah	Okay, sweetie.

As much as I enjoyed my text relationship with Mitch, talking to him on the phone was intoxicating. His voice was so deep and sexy, and he sounded genuine. If we had talked more often, it might have moved our relationship along faster. But he always seemed to be on the move while we were on the phone—I often heard car doors closing, keys rattling, or water running, and he was interrupted by someone every time. So our conversations were direct and brief, unless there was an issue we needed to discuss. We obliged each other if one of us needed to talk about family matters or work, and that was fine. But I wanted to stay in the love zone with this man. I did not want things to become a dumping ground filled with negativity. So while I was ready to meet in person, texting had a special value to me and kept me satisfied. Once again, however, I did not hear from him for days. Finally, he texted me with "Hey, boo," and I responded by asking him to call me.

"What's up, boo?" he asked.

"What's up with you is my question. Am I wrong to expect to hear from you on a consistent basis?"

"No, boo, you can expect things, but that doesn't mean they will always happen. I told you from the start I have a lot of things going on."

Okay, Mitch, I see where this is going, so I will not hold you any longer. Talk to you later."

"Fine, boo. Bye."

Mitch	God made me for you. Open your soul, and let me in, boo. "Funtyme 911."
Karah	Is your soul open?
Mitch	Yes, it is, but only for you. "Funtyme 911."
Mitch	So, what are we going to do? "Funtyme 911."
Karah	Capture each other's hearts, I hope, but I must admit I am a little disturbed.
Mitch	Why? "Funtyme 911."
Karah	Too many sudden absences.
Mitch	Girl, I'm working so much you would not believe. Sometimes I fall asleep and then get up early in the morning and do it all over again. "Funtyme 911."
Karah	I understand. I've been there. I'm just in a different place now.
Mitch	Be patient, boo. I'm going to love you like you never imagined! "Funtyme 911."

Karah	If not for my relationship with God … maybe I'd be reluctant or afraid. I prayed for my king and specifically asked that he would adore me.
Karah	God asked me to prepare myself—my heart, mind, body, and soul. I did that, and I am ready.
Mitch	I prayed as well, and God sent me you, and I miss you dearly every day. "Funtyme 911."
Karah	No dating for two years.
Karah	The next man who touches me must be very special.
Mitch	Baby, I am special; we are special, but I will not touch you until you give me the green light! You have the key to my heart! "Funtyme 911."
Karah	Oh, you have the green light. LOL.
Karah	I can feel you. I can close my eyes and feel your hands all over me.
Karah	I know it's going to be very emotional for me
Mitch	I just want to hold you all night long. "Funtyme 911."
Karah	Yes … yes, please do.
Karah	Hold me and take away my doubts and fears.
Mitch	I plan to. "Funtyme 911."
Karah	I'll brace myself.
Mitch	Good morning, sunshine! "Funtyme 911."
Karah	Morning.
Mitch	I felt like I was holding you all night. "Funtyme 911."
Karah	You keep saying you'll just hold me. Are you so sure you'll have that much control?
Karah	I am a very soft and sensual woman … and I will not want you to have so much control.
Mitch	I'll be a total gentleman. "Funtyme 911."
Karah	Are you sure you can handle loving me?

Karah	I will be squirming all over the place.
Karah	Two years—let's not forget that. LOL.
Mitch	That is a long time and shows the discipline you have. "Funtyme 911."
Mitch	I will make passionate, explosive love to you. "Funtyme 911."
Karah	That will be the key to opening the floodgates.
Karah	I don't want to be all reserved.
Karah	I want you ... to take me there.
Mitch	I'll take it nice and slow; that's what you need. "Funtyme 911."
Karah	Absolutely not! LOL.
Mitch	I'll do whatever you ask me to do, love. "Funtyme 911."
Karah	What I want is for you to use every skill you have. Unlock every compartment I have, and set me free.
Karah	Then let me sleep in your arms. When I awake, you will be right there, telling me you love and adore me.
Mitch	And we will live happily ever after. "Funtyme 911."
Karah	Missing you.
Mitch	You are my sunshine. "Funtyme 911."
Karah	Damn ... damn ... damn ... I'm caught up. I haven't heard from you in days, but now I'm smiling like a damn fool!
Mitch	Let me see. "Funtyme 911."
Karah	See what?
Mitch	Your sexy face. "Funtyme 911."
Karah	Oh, how sweet. OK.
Mitch	I miss you very much. "Funtyme 911."
Mitch	I need to see you. "Funtyme 911."
Karah	OK.
Mitch	Ah, excuse me? "Funtyme 911."
Mitch	Karah? "Funtyme 911."

Karah	Yes.
Mitch	Are you ignoring me? "Funtyme 911."
Karah	Maybe.
Mitch	I said I need to see you. "Funtyme 911."
Karah	I said yes two days ago. Now I'm not ready. Every time I get close, you disappear. I don't feel comfortable.
Mitch	Girl, we've been texting and talking for almost three months. It's time for us to meet. I have to insist ... or you will never agree. No more thinking about it. Your choice of place and time. Let me know ... now. "Funtyme 911."
Karah	Okay, Boo. Tomorrow. 3:00. Downtown in front of the courthouse.
Mitch	Wonderful. I'm there. See you tomorrow. Do not change your mind on me. "Funtyme 911."
Karah	I will not change my mind. I promise. See you tomorrow.

After three months of texting and talking on the phone, it was finally time to meet. Mitch wasn't taking no for an answer, and I really wanted to take a chance with him. I was still reluctant; I realized that a few things could go wrong. The chemistry between us concerned me, as well as the fact that we just might not like each other. Most important, however, was my safety. I did not want to end up in the news. I was always very responsible, and I had to admit that this was very risky. I kept thinking about my first internet encounter, and even though it was in a public place, his behavior was over the top and embarrassing, to say the least. So I had to apply every bit of caution I could. I had to have some control over the situation, so I asked Mitch to meet me downtown on a Sunday. I just wanted to be in the open with him. The weather wasn't too cold, so I figured there would be a lot of people walking around, and I would feel safe. I just wanted to walk around town and talk and maybe get something to eat.

I got up, as usual. I felt calm and didn't go through special preparations. I put on jeans, a red sweater, and boots. I grabbed a jacket in case the temperature dropped in the evening. I didn't feel nervous at first. I got there early, and evidently so did he. At exactly three o'clock, I opened my car door, and the door of a car across the parking lot also opened. My knees trembled as I saw a male figure emerge. He made some adjustments to his clothing and then reached inside the car to get something—a cap. He put it on his head, closed the door, and walked toward me. I took a deep breath, closed my door, and walked to the front of my car. I just stood there as he approached. As soon as we could see each other's face, a big smile broke through.

"So you're Ms. Karah, the woman who kept me waiting for three whole months."

"Yes, that would be me."

"Well, pretty lady, I'm glad I waited."

"And so am I."

Mitch and I walked and talked, sometimes quite playfully. We stopped for burgers and talked some more. Darkness started to fall, and he walked me back to my car. We gave each other a hug and said our goodbyes.

"Oh wait," he said suddenly. "Almost forgot." He ran over to his car and reached into the back seat. After concealing something behind his back as he walked back to me, he handed me a package. "I told you I had your Christmas present. Open it!"

Carefully, I unwrapped the box. It was a beautiful porcelain doll. I took her out. She was a black girl with brown eyes and short curly hair. She was outfitted in red pants and a jacket with a white collar. She wore shiny black heels that matched her belt. I was absolutely blown away. I hugged him long and tight.

"Thank you," I said. "She is beautiful."

"As soon as I saw her, I thought about you," he said. "Keep her safe; she is very fragile—and quite expensive," he added with a laugh.

"I will, and I will treasure her always."

Later that evening, we started texting again.

Mitch	Hey, I didn't scare you away, did I? "Funtyme 911."
Karah	No, of course not.
Mitch	That wasn't so bad, was it? "Funtyme 911."

Karah	No, it was very nice, and I love my doll. Thank you again; she is beautiful.
Mitch	So what did you think about me? How did I look? Was I what you expected? "Funtyme 911."
Karah	Yes, I had a similar picture of you in mind. Plus, we have shared quite a few photos. Now you—what did you think of me?
Mitch	Well, honestly … LOL. "Funtyme 911."
Karah	Honestly what? Go on.
Mitch	No, I was just fooling around. You are all I expected and much more. Your pictures didn't lie, and you have a banging body. "Funtyme 911."
Karah	LOL. Well, thank you, and you are very sexy. Got that bad-boy swag … like Denzel.
Mitch	Oh no, not Denzel. "Funtyme 911."
Karah	Yes, I always wanted my own Denzel.
Karah	So where do we go from here?
Mitch	Everywhere … together. "Funtyme 911."

We continued to meet around town and take in the sights and have coffee. Mitch didn't drink, and I didn't want to drink alone, so we just grabbed a sandwich or pizza and enjoyed each other's company. I was excited to have someone in my life, but honestly, it lacked the chemistry I'd expected. Moreover, he wasn't refined. He didn't mention fine dining or anything upscale. When he told me he didn't dance, I was stunned.

"How is that even possible?" I asked. "What do you do at the club?"

"Well, boo, I just walk around and look good."

"What about when you take a lady out?"

"I make it clear I don't dance."

"You didn't make it clear to me."

"Well, it never came up. That's why I'm making it clear now."

Disappointment could not begin to express how I felt. Still baffled, I asked, "Are you willing to learn?"

He just looked at me and laughed. "Sure, boo, whatever you want."

This guy has zero class, I thought. I was not willing to settle for just having a man. I wanted the man God had for me, plain and simple. I'd been in relationships that were okay, not over the top, but there was nothing like the love I'd shared with K. C.

We were stationed in Germany, which created the ambiance. Everything was love, and that set the standard for the kind of man I desired in my life. Trust became a major issue, though, so our relationship didn't last. Still, I knew in my heart I would never be totally satisfied without someone similar to him.

The opposite was true in my relationship with my husband. Trust drove the direction of the relationship, and romance took a back seat. George and I loved each other, and we were both committed to the marriage. We only had ten years of marriage, however, before he died of that dreadful disease.

Now I had two standards for the kind of love I needed. I hoped to find a mate who possessed both. *That* would be the man of my dreams. Instead, I had neither. That doll was the only bit of class I'd seen in Mitch. Still, maybe if we had the right chemistry between us, it would be OK. We could be great lovers and friends. If not, this relationship was a complete waste of time. So I had to know, and the sooner the better.

The next evening, I was talking to Mitch on the phone and asked him to spend the night with me. He agreed and asked for the address.

"I'm not comfortable with you coming to my house," I said. "I prefer getting a hotel room." I still felt I had to control the situation, even though I cared for him and believed he cared for me. I knew we both would be more comfortable in a neutral environment. This was our first romantic encounter, and I wanted it to be special.

I brought a sandwich platter, chips, cookies, soda, and wine (two bottles). I had a teddy, but I did not put it on. I showered and slipped into a sexy, slinky sundress and waited patiently. He called when he got in the area, and I gave him the name of the hotel and the room number. Soon afterward, I heard a knock at the door, and I greeted him with a smile.

"Good evening, Ms. Karah," he said as he walked past me with some clothes on a hanger. He hung up his clothes and put down his overnight bag. "So how was your day?" he asked as he looked in the mirror, picking at his face.

I sat calmly, sipping on my wine. "Fine," I replied. I was observing his every move and already getting a bad vibe.

"I need to take a shower," he said.

"By all means," I replied.

I wasn't feeling any chemistry, and my mind was running wild. He didn't hug or kiss me—unbelievable. He stayed in the shower so long I was getting pissed off, but I just watched the news and waited. When he came out, he casually came over and sat next to me.

"Now I'm fresh and clean," he said. "I can hold my sweet lady all night long. Girl, I was so happy when you said to come spend the night. I did a Tiger Woods fist pump and a Michael Jackson spin. You don't know how happy that made me. I wanted to ask so many times, but I just couldn't. I don't want to do anything to push you away." He moved onto the bed and patted the spot next to him. "Come lie in my arms."

I turned on some music and squeezed up next to him. The fragrance of his body was so alluring. It smelled like chocolate and musk, and it was intoxicating. I just lay on his chest and closed my eyes as he caressed my face ever so gently.

"Are you my baby?" he asked.

"Yes," I replied.

He gazed into my eyes, squinting as though he was looking for the peephole to my soul. His hands were soft yet masculine, and I wanted to feel them all over my body. I eased up and out of my dress. I wanted him to feel as much skin as possible. Beyoncé performing "Drunk in Love" guided my actions. *Flawless*, however, was not the word to describe the night.

The chemistry between us sucked; this was not the love I desired. I knew in my heart that God had a different mate designed for me, and chemistry would be the first sign. Still, I accepted the way things were.

After that night, Mitch and I continued to share texts and talk and get together every chance we could. We were lovers and friends, and that worked for the next nine months.

One morning, FedEx brought a package. It was my book, and I was elated. I called Mitch, screaming with joy.

"Mitch! I just got the copy of my book!"

"Oh really? That's good, ba." He hesitated for a moment and then said, "Hey, let me holla at you later."

"Okay. Talk to you later."

It was two days later when I heard from Mitch, and even then, there was no further mention of my book. I was disappointed, and that was not good. There is no way the man for me would not have been more excited for me.

A few more days passed, and he disappeared again. I just could not imagine what excuse he would offer, but I had to ask. So I called him.

"Where you been?" I asked without preamble. "I haven't heard from you in a few days."

"I've been busy. You know my work. Sometimes it's like that—long days, work and sleep."

"I was just wondering why you never said anything else about my book."

"What else did you want me to say?"

"Well, maybe 'Can I see it? Let's go celebrate.' This is a pretty big deal for me."

"Yeah, well, it can't always be about you."

"Oh really? Wow, that's pretty harsh, but okay. Bye."

"Hold up. So what? Now you're pissed off?"

"Not really, but I've said all I have to say."

"Cool. I'll text you later."

"Whatever. Bye."

There is something wrong with this fool, I thought. Why wouldn't he be excited for me? And now, suddenly, he can't call or text? I just couldn't get that out of my head. Immediately, my feelings for him changed. He'd text me; I wouldn't reply. Over and over his texts went unanswered. The phone rang, but I would not answer. My anger was getting more intense. He wasn't my mate—that became very clear to me. "Funtyme 911"—yep, it sure was. Now it was time to move on. I was no longer willing to accept his behavior or to keep telling him what I wanted in a man. All the molding and shaping eventually would have a created a totally different person. He might change the things I complained about, but the real person would always be inside. There would be a battle between two identities, and I'd never know which one would emerge. No, I wasn't going to allow it.

The man for me would be sensitive to my needs. Our love would be natural, and our goals for life would be similar. We simply did not have enough in common. He was dedicated to his Harley bike club and his job. Then there was the church and the kids. He could barely squeeze me in. I'd told him over and over that I would *not* be squeezed in.

Letting go would not be easy. We'd tried breaking up a few times, but we each insisted on getting back together, primarily because it was convenient. Not this time. I was ready for a solid relationship, and this was only preventing that from happening. So I focused on all the negatives and eased my way right out of that relationship. I never looked back.

Mitch	Can I come see you tonight? "Funtyme 911."
Karah	No, I'm not interested in seeing you anymore.
Mitch	Why? "Funtyme 911."
Karah	Things are not the same with us.
Mitch	Let me see you so we can talk. "Funtyme 911."
Karah	No.
Mitch	You are my queen. "Funtyme 911."
Mitch	I adore you. "Funtyme 911."
Mitch	Let me see you, please. "Funtyme 911."
Mitch	I want to marry you. "Funtyme 911."
Karah	For us to be godly people, there must be something spiritual between us. There isn't.

Mitch	We can do better. "Funtyme 911."
Mitch	Let me see you, please. "Funtyme 911."
Karah	No, you don't respect whatever this is that we have.
Mitch	I just want to hold you. "Funtyme 911."
Karah	Why?
Mitch	You complete me. "Funtyme 911."
Karah	You don't deserve me.
Mitch	I'll make it up to you. "Funtyme 911."
Karah	No ... I will not try again.
Mitch	Well, since you will not allow me to see you, can you send me a picture? "Funtyme 911."
Karah	Absolutely not!
Mitch	Okay. "Funtyme 911."
Mitch	Can I come? "Funtyme 911."
Karah	No.
Mitch	See you @ 8? "Funtyme 911."
Karah	No.
Karah	I don't want to see you anymore.
Mitch	I'm coming to see you, Karah. "Funtyme 911."
Karah	No!
Mitch	Morning. "Funtyme 911."
Karah	GM.
Mitch	Need to see you. "Funtyme 911."
Karah	Please stop texting me. I'm not for you, and you are not for me. It's all good ... big mistake.
Mitch	Like you tell me—block the number, then! "Funtyme 911."
Karah	No, just in case you want to apologize for being an asshole first.
Mitch	I miss you, Karah; please don't do this. "Funtyme 911."

Karah	It's already done. I gave you the easiest opportunity. Just friends … no games necessary, but you … OMG.
Mitch	Let me call you. "Funtyme 911."
Karah	No! I don't want to talk. I am done with this.
Mitch	Do you have someone new? "Funtyme 911."
Karah	It shouldn't matter to you. But I don't change interests so easily.
Mitch	Morning. "Funtyme 911."
Karah	OMG.
Mitch	Can I come see you tomorrow? "Funtyme 911."
Karah	No. Just let this fade away.
Karah	I am no longer interested in us.
Mitch	You don't mean that. "Funtyme 911."
Karah	Yes, I do. But all is well. I've learned a lot from this relationship. Listen carefully to the words of this song— I'm sending you Chrisette Michele's "Love Won't Leave Me Out."
Mitch	Karah, stop. I love you! "Funtyme 911."
Karah	Well, I'm sorry, but … you should have kept it real. Now I don't want your love or anything else. Just let it go.
Mitch	I can't. "Funtyme 911."
Karah	You will eventually!

It didn't take long for Mitch to fully understand that I was serious. Once he did, our conversations went far to the left. We were rude to each other, and that annoyed both of us. It reminded me of kids having temper tantrums. I guess that's what it was. That can happen when things don't go your way. We each started saying things that were not heartfelt—at least, I don't believe they were, but they were still hurtful. He called me old, and I called him young, dumb, and full of …

It was just time to let go. I didn't think Mitch was a bad person; he just wasn't the man for me, and I was not going to settle for what he was offering. As for my loneliness, just like before, I asked God to give me peace.

"Father, if this is not your will for me, then give me peace. I don't want to be tossing and turning all night and feeling lonely. Thank you for your blessings. In Jesus's name, amen.

9

Time to Retreat

It had been a very long year, and I still missed Mitch. I needed to get away, so I call Naomi, now stationed in Hawaii. She invited me to come over for some much-needed rest and relaxation. I was packed and out that door before she could finish her sentence.

Arriving in Honolulu was much different this time. I wasn't a soldier, and I wasn't a tourist. I had been there several times, and Naomi consistently reminded me to act like a local, and this time I felt like one.

"Karah, where are you? Did you get your bags?"

"Yeah, girlie, I'm outside."

"Where, girlie? I don't see you."

"I'm right under the AA sign."

"Oh, I see you."

She pulled over to the curb, and I jumped in.

"Girlie, where are your bags?" she asked.

"This is it," I replied as I held up the strap to my carry-on.

"Now that's local-style," she said as she pulled away. "Girlie, I thought I was going to be late. These freaking tourists drive slowly. Guess they didn't get the memo that I was picking up my BBF—*best* best friend. They're all just cruising like it's Sunday morning. So how was your flight?"

"Everything was great," I answered. "Perfect. Now I just want to have some fun."

"Oh, don't worry!"

Her tone caused me to reply, "Okay, girlie, go slow. My ass is old. These achy bones can't handle what they used to."

"Well, girl, I can't make that promise. We are going to get fit while you are here. This will be your Hawaiian fitness retreat with your BBF. We are going snorkeling and hiking, attending hot yoga and spin classes, beachcombing, and maybe even parasailing!"

"OK, hold up—ground or water. Let's draw that line right now."

We were just laughing along the way.

"I'm so glad to have you here," Naomi said, "I have so much to show you."

The area had grown since I was last there, and I could not believe the traffic. I guessed it was nothing compared to New Jersey and New York, though, because Naomi was whipping through traffic and fussing at the other drivers the entire time. When we got to her neighborhood, I was flabbergasted. It was as if we had traveled into a new dimension—extravagant homes, well-manicured lawns, people walking their dogs and jogging everywhere. Not a piece of paper was on the ground anywhere. She pulled up to the garage and waited as the door went up. Inside was all neat and organized.

"Wow, Naomi, everything's dress right dress. Looks like a soldier did this."

"Girl, I know," she replied. "It's in my blood." Naomi grabbed bags from the front seat, back seat, and then the trunk.

"Let me help you," I offered.

"No, girlie, I got it. This is a way of life for me. I'm multitasking my ass off." She stopped for a moment and then said, "Watch this step. I told that fix-it man this tile was broken, and my ass was gonna slip, and he was gonna have to take care of me. I think that's what he wants because he ain't fixed that shit yet."

We went out the back door of the garage into her private courtyard. A privacy fence on each side, barbecue grill, and lawn chairs decorated the patio.

"Oh my, this yard is just screaming garden party," I said.

"Yes, girlie, cocktail time."

As soon as she opened the door, the dogs nearly knocked her down. Their excitement was overflowing, like little children screaming, *Mommy, mommy.*

"Hey, Kaiya. Hey, Autumn. Did you guys miss me? This is Auntie Karah; you remember her. Yeah, you do, don't you? Auntie Karah's going to be staying here, so be on your best behavior. Karah, these dogs are so freaking smart. Last week—girl, just put your stuff down; I'll show you around in a second—last week I picked up some ribs from Remo's, my favorite rib place. I was drooling for those ribs, but I got home and realized I had left my link at work. Girl, I was pissed, but I had to have that link. After all, I was on call. So I drove my ass all the way back to Hickam. I rushed back home, drooling for my ribs. I walked in the door, and the first thing I saw was the Styrofoam plate on the floor."

"Oh no!" I exclaimed.

"Karah, the freaking dogs somehow they got their fat little asses up there and got that plate of ribs." She shook her finger at one of the dogs, saying, "Kaiya, I know it was you." Then she turned back to me. "Girlie, they got my ribs and did not leave not one bone. Not one. No gristle, no slaw, no bread; it was all gone. Girl, I was so freaking mad, and those dogs knew it. They both took off upstairs, and that's where they stayed until they had to poop. They had to come down then because they knew if they pooped or peed in this house, Shelly would take them to the pound. So Karah, keep any food or stuff up here on this counter. Surely they can't get up here; if they do, girlie, I'm leaving. They can have this house. I'm gone."

"Girl, you keep me laughing. That's why I love to hang out with you."

"Let's have some coffee and catch up, and then I'll show you around. Karah, this is the best coffee ever. It is locally grown for locals. Not sold on the market. Plus, I love my coffee press. It gives coffee a whole new flavor."

We enjoyed our coffee and conversation, and I realized just how refreshing it was to be with her. Her personality was exuberant. We laughed and talked for hours about the past, the present, and the future. After showing me to my room, she encouraged me to get a good night's sleep because we had to climb Koko Head early, and I would need my energy.

The next morning I got up early, had my breakfast, and took my medication. I also had my favorite energy drink. I would never make it without that. We packed a few goodies in a backpack and off we went. Her sister Kay was meeting us there. We got to the park, and before we reached the start of the climb, Kay pointed to movement on the mountain in front of us.

"See, Karah? That's it," she said in her thick Hawaiian accent.

Instantly, I got a headache. "No way!" I replied.

"Yes, girl. It's not so bad. Right, Naomi? Looks worse than what it is, yeah."

Kay sounded convincing. I took them at their lying words, but before I got a third of the way up, I was struggling. Each step was about a foot step up to the next. Each step consisted of a wooden platform about twelve inches deep, then a patch of gravel, then the next step up. So I had to step up onto the wooden board and then take a half step before I could reach the next step up. This was annoying and challenging for me. I noticed a dirt path to the right of the steps, and although it was partially covered with brush, it was a better option for me. I made that work for a while, and it was easier on my knees. I could see Naomi and Kay up ahead. They were just chatting and strolling along, while I was already exhausted.

Then about halfway up the climb, my dirt path ran out, and I faced my ultimate fear. Suddenly, there was a bridge. No step up, no sides—just planks across a huge gap in the earth. A ditch, a gulch, a hole—call it what you will, but I was petrified. I stood there just staring as people went around me. I couldn't move. I don't know how much time passed, maybe ten minutes or more. I could no longer see Naomi or Kay. *Okay*, I said to myself, *how do I conquer this obstacle? Think … think … come on, Karah. Think. You can do this. Okay, crawl.* I got down on all fours. Now more people were staring, and some said encouraging words, but one guy pulled out his phone.

I got past my fear long enough to say, "You'd better not take my picture."

"Okay, okay, but this is too funny," he replied.

Okay, Karah, I told myself, *focus. It's only a few feet. Crawl. Shit! That hurt my knees. Oh no, don't look down. Come on, girl, crawl, crawl. Almost there; ignore the pain.* My arms were shaking. I wanted to cry. *Keep going; you can't go back; keep going; almost there.* Finally—*OMG fuck, that hurt.* At the point, before I'd even stood up, an Asian girl was standing over me.

"Are you Karah?" she said. "Excuse me, are you Karah?"

"Yes," I answered.

"Your friends asked me to check on you."

Without thinking, I blurted out, "I have no friends. I have no freaking friends."

"You can do it," she replied, almost pleadingly. "Here—take this." She handed me some Gummi Bears. "This will give you some energy."

"Thank you," I replied, looking at the wooden steps. "Now where will I get the courage?" She went along her way. I ate the candy, and it did give me energy. I climbed, but I was only three-quarters up. I could see Naomi already coming back down.

"Almost there, Karah," she said gleefully.

"Girl, I don't know if I can take another step."

"Well, turn around, and we can come back and try another day."

"What? Absolutely not; I am doing this today."

Step by painful step, I struggled my way to the top. The view was magnificent. I felt relieved, but I was exhausted, and all I could think of was that I had to get back down!

Going back down was worse. Every muscle I'd used to go up had to be used to come down. The step down was long, so I had to use my thigh muscles a lot. I had to put the weight of my body on my left thigh to control the impact of my right foot coming down on the step. Then the weight was all on my right thigh as I controlled the impact of my left. I was not up for this challenge.

I had only taken a few steps when I decided that spider-walking would be better. My arms were well rested, and I could give my hips and thighs a break. So I sat down, slid to the edge of the step, and gently stepped down to the next step. Foot, foot, hand, hand—it wasn't pretty, but I had no choice. I was doing okay and was halfway down—then came that freaking bridge. As I stood, trying to figure this out and get my courage up again, I heard someone say, "Maybe you shouldn't do the bridge. Just go under those bushes over there; there's a path."

"Thank you so much!" I replied. *I am going to strangle Naomi,* I thought. *She never mentioned this freaking path.*

I finally made it down, but it was a challenge to reach the car. For the next week, every step I took, every move I made, reminded me of my embarrassing Koko Head performance. I could only pray that no one had taken a picture or video of me at my worst hour.

One morning we decided to go to the flea market, which stretched around the Aloha Stadium. It was early, not too hot, and I felt pretty good. The pain from Koko Head was going away, but the bruise to my ego was still as painful as if it had happened that day. We'd been walking for a while when we came across an old Hawaiian man selling coconuts. He cut the top off and gave me a straw. The coconut water was so refreshing; I felt revived immediately.

We continued along, and as we ventured into one of the booths, I was startled by a huge picture of Koko Head—it made my heart skip a beat. Did I now have PTSD from that climb?

"Aloha, sista," said the man running the booth.

"Aloha, braddah," I replied.

"You like the picture?" he asked. "That's Koko Head. Many people climb there every day."

"Yeah, braddah, I know. I did the climb last week."

"Did you make it all the way, sista?"

"Yeah, but it was painful."

"Way to go!" he replied enthusiastically. "I tried, but I had to turn around about halfway up. I still have not seen the top for myself."

Naomi had been trying to reassure me by telling me that same thing over and over, but I guess I was in too much pain. Today was different. Today, I graciously said thank you, and I felt proud.

That evening we gathered in the kitchen and made salad to have with our rotisserie chicken. I heard a key in the door.

"Who is that?" Naomi playfully asked the dogs. "Who's that, Kaiya?"

I was surprised to see Mama gracefully enter the kitchen.

"Hi, Mama," I said excitedly as I stood up. I was intrigued by this Hawaiian lady. The fact that she was over eighty years old and still driving was a sign of her resilience. She greeted us each with a kiss on the cheek. Speaking in her thick Hawaiian accent, she talked about her drive over.

"The traffic … awful!" she said, shaking her head. "People drive so fast."

Naomi looked at me. "That's who's cruising like its Sunday morning, girlie. Eighty-year-old Hawaiian people, just like Mom."

"I want to go to the VFW," Mama said.

"Mom, that's too far," Naomi said.

"No, I go there every Friday night."

"Sounds like fun," I said.

"Naomi, come wit'."

"No, Mom, I don't want to go that far. I'm tired."

"I'll drive. Come wit'," she said.

"No, Mom."

"OK, Karah, come wit'," she said.

"Sure, I'd love to go," I replied.

"Naomi, come with me and Karah. We want stay late."

"Oh, Mom," Naomi said with a sigh, "just for a little while."

"I'm so excited!" I said. Mama still getting out and deserved our support.

"What time is it?" Mama asked.

"Five o'clock," I replied.

"OK, we'll leave at seven."

The drive was long, and the traffic was still heavy. Naomi drove, but when we got close, she had to ask Mom for directions.

"Turn here," she said.

"Where, here? Oh, my God, Mom, a little sooner next time. Jeez!" she said.

We all laughed. We traveled briefly through a neighborhood before we came to the guard shack, which looked abandoned. We parked next to what looked like an old wharf. Once inside the VFW building, I realized that the wharf was a part of the club, so we were right next to the water. It was very nice. It was a long pier with a dance floor at the right and tables in front and to the left. I was standing there, looking out at the ocean, when I realized that Mama had continued walking. The place was crowded, but without hesitation, Mama walked up to a table where a couple was sitting. After talking briefly with the man, Mama gestured for us to come on over. We grabbed extra chairs and joined the couple.

"Tu-Tu," the waitress said to Mama, "I'm so glad you made it."

Then others kept saying "Tu-Tu, Tu-Tu" to her. I asked Naomi what it meant, and she told me it was a term of endearment, meaning Grandma. I soon realized that Mama was a regular here. Many people knew her, and she was very comfortable with them. A band set up on the corner of the dance floor, and as soon as they started to play, it was crowded with people. A young, handsome guy came over and took Mama by the hand, and there she was, out on the dance floor, having a ball. To my surprise, Mama then came to get me, and I was honored. She wanted me to join her on the dance floor, and I did.

After a series of songs, I was exhausted, and rejoined Naomi at the table. She had ordered some garlic shrimp and fries and our favorite Hawaiian cocktail, the Lava Flow. This girl was the best at entertaining me. She had my best interests in mind, and she never forgot the things I liked. I loved her for it. As we sat there watching Mama, who never left the dance floor, someone tapped me on the shoulder. It was a girl. I thought she was with the guy who had led Mama onto the dance floor, but I no longer saw him. People were dancing and having fun in groups, not coupled off, as I was accustomed to seeing. The girl never said a word; she just pointed to the dance floor. It was a little strange to me, but what the heck; I went. When the song ended, I tried to leave, but she kept dancing around me. Finally, I made my escape and went back to the table.

Naomi was laughing so hard. "Girlie, she likes you!"

"No, girl, stop. She just wants me to have a good time."

We started talking with the couple at the table, who said they were glad Mama had asked to join them. Then there was a tap on my shoulder again; it was the same girl.

"No," I said.

She pointed to the dance floor and then made a praying-hand gesture. Naomi was trying to hold back her laughter.

"No," I repeated, "we're about to leave."

She put up an index finger, waggling it back and forth.

I understood her gesture to mean "just one more," so I danced again, but this time, from the dance floor, I gave my own gestures to Naomi.

Let's go now! I kept mouthing to Naomi as I pointed at the door.

Finally, we got Mama and danced our way to the exit. That girl was still dancing her ass off as we left.

For the next few weeks Naomi took me on unforgettable adventures. Her teenage niece came over from DC, and that encouraged even more outings. When she took me and her niece to the mermaid hole, I never could have imagined it being so terrifying. We went to a remote part of the island of which only the locals had knowledge. The hard stares we received as we got out of the car concerned me a little. Many locals expressed disapproval of the tourists taking over the island. But Naomi and her niece were Hawaiian, and they were not concerned at all.

We climbed over the jagged rocks until we got to a hole in the rocks. We peered down into the hole, which was a gouged-out area that led to the ocean. Water was crashing in and rapidly flowing back out to the ocean. It was not a violent or huge action, but the continued movement was breaking the gravel down from the wall of the cave.

It was interesting to look at it, but when Naomi started climbing down into the hole, panic set in. I expressed concern, but this was a smart girl, and if she was willing to go in, surely it was safe. Still, I just watched. After a few minutes, my discomfort returned, and I urged her to get out.

"Okay, Karah!" she yelled. As she attempted to climb out, her feet couldn't get a grip on the slippery rock wall.

"Auntie, reach up this side," her niece yelled down.

She did, but that did not work either. I tried to pull her up by her hand, but she was too heavy, and she still could not get a grip with her feet. We all started to panic. All sorts of scenarios played out in my head.

Then her niece decided that the best thing was for her to get in the hole too and boost Naomi up. Once Naomi was out, the two of us could get her niece out, as she was lighter. No discussion—she jumped in. I sat down and braced my feet on the inside edge of the hole. They struggled, trying to find the best way to make this exit happen. All the while, I was thinking through the next option—where would I go for help?

Finally, I heard the niece say, "Okay, Auntie, one, two, three." Naomi stepped on to her back and was halfway out of the hole. I pulled on her arm, and she struggled, pushing her feet from several spots on the wall. Finally, she was out. Her niece was a little easier, but this was a little too close to a disaster for me. From that point on, I was not getting into any water on the island of Oahu.

For the remainder of my time in Hawaii, we explored the island by eating local foods and taking pictures. The North Shore was Naomi's favorite place to get local food. I was still impressed with the effects of the coconut water, so we went there often to get the freshest on the island. But for relaxation we went to the new resort on the mountain side. Disney had a hotel there, and there were six lagoons. We sipped Mai Tais and Lava Flows by the lagoons, and my stress level dropped rapidly. I was feeling great and continued to explore the island, but my time was running out. I had one more weekend there, and I wanted to spend it in Waikiki.

One of her nieces danced the hula and was performing in Waikiki. It was perfect. We attended her show and were amazed by her performance. Many local girls danced the hula, but she was the star of this show. Afterward, they took me to a club called Rum Fire, right on the beach. We sat on the patio, relaxing and watching the waves crashing against the shore. Some waves were big, and people walking along the shore got splashed. Naomi's two nieces went inside and playfully danced together on the dance floor. They laughed and carried on as each did her brief dance. I noticed a guy approach them and extend his hand toward the girls. They blew him off and continued to carry on with each other.

I could see the disappointment on his face as he walked away to rejoin the group of guys standing near the floor. I could not resist the opportunity to rescue him. I boldly walked out on the dance floor and started to dance right next to him. He joined me. As we danced around, I introduced myself. He told me his name and that he was from Australia.

"We are here on vacation," he said.

"Oh, what kind of work do you do?" I asked.

"We make elevators."

"Elevators!"

"Yes, my dad owns the business. Those are my brothers." He pointed them out. "Can you guess which one is the oldest?"

"No," I replied.

"Aw, come on, take a guess."

I pointed to one of the guys.

He laughed. "No, he's the youngest. I'm the oldest. I have to take care of them—keep them out of trouble."

We laughed as we looked in his brothers' direction. Soon, they joined us.

"What kind of lie is he telling you?" one of them asked me.

They appeared to be good guys, and when the song ended, I introduced them to my friends. They got along very well, and for the remainder of the night, we enjoyed each other's company. We even exchanged contact information and agreed to stay in touch. Before we left, they thanked me for the best time they'd had since arriving in Hawaii.

My time was almost over, but Naomi had something else on her mind.

"Girlie, go slip on some yoga gear, and let's take a ride. We have time for one more adventure. Hot yoga is just what you need to relax your muscles before you leave on Tuesday."

This sounded like fun, so I did not object. To my knowledge, yoga was slow, easy movements—and how hot could it be?

Kay met us there, and we quickly joined the class. Since this was my first time, I went to the back of the class, despite their insistence that I stay next to them. It was nice and easy from the start, and I enjoyed the stretches. I was following the instructions with ease—and then the instructor suddenly picked up the pace.

"Everybody get on the floor," she commanded. "Lie on your backs, hands to your sides, feet flat on the floor. Breathe deep. Stand up. Reach for the sky. Hold it. Now bend at the waist, and touch the floor. Now push-up position—hold it. Flat on your stomachs; roll over. Flat on your backs. Feet flat on the floor. OK, let's repeat the series."

You have got *to be kidding me*, I thought.

"Reach up, stretch, stretch, bend at the waist. Touch the floor. Push-up position, hold it, and hold it. Flat on your stomachs. Legs and arms stretched out. Legs up, down, up, down."

At that point I just lay on my mat, and that's where I stayed until the session was over.

Naomi's adventures had to come to an end. I was scheduled to leave that evening. Naomi made sure I left the island with a treat bag. I was sad to leave but knew I would see Naomi soon because she was being reassigned to the New York City area again. I said my goodbyes and left Hawaii feeling relaxed and at peace.

Once I got on the plane, however, I immediately started having problems. My hips and back kept cramping up. My feet were still swollen. I was so uncomfortable. I was twisting and turning the entire flight. I had to take more pain medication to endure the ten-hour flight. It was obvious I had pushed myself too far. It was hard to resist Naomi's adventures, but as with everything else in my life now, there had to be limits. Still, she would be excited to explore less grueling choices. Additionally, if I was going to fly, it had to be first class.

10

BBNC

I was excited to get home. I loved to travel, but it was exhausting. I got a rental car and drove from the airport. I'd asked Baby-boy to pick me up from the local rental car place. When he got there, I could immediately tell something was different. He greeted me but not with the exceptionally long, tight hug he was famous for. Everyone had experience that sometimes annoying expression of his love. Mama used to say, "Okay, Okay, Baby-boy, stop now."

So I was expecting that I'd need to tell him to let me go and put me down. Instead, he gave me a casual "Hi, Mother" as he grabbed my suitcases. He drove the five miles without any small talk. He answered every question I asked with short, direct responses.

"How have you been?"

"Okay."

"Did you miss me?"

"Yes."

"Have you seen your sisters and brother?"

"No."

This was noticeably out of character. I had been gone two weeks, and this was not his usual reaction when I returned. *He came to get me right from work, so maybe he's just tired,* I thought. He was so much like his dad—silly, comical, and always entertaining. Unfortunately, the loss of his father had an effect on his personality, and he sometimes seemed scornful. I could often see it in his eyes. Pain and confusion had hijacked his mind, and he was plagued with burning questions that could never be answered. I knew that heart-wrenching place. I'd been there throughout my childhood, especially as I fought for peace of mind regarding the loss of my own dad.

Baby-boy was also much like me and Mama. Our artistic nature could keep us locked away for days as we focused on projects. Nothing would be wrong; we just enjoyed keeping to ourselves. I remember mama calling me over to see her latest creations. She'd tell me how she'd messed up a number of times but then, she'd proudly say, "I finally got it." People were amazed to see some of the things she crafted, often for her own convenience.

"I was tired of looking for that remote control, and most of the time it was under the bed covers. Now it has a place of its own," she once said as she showed off her special pouch for the remote that hung conveniently next to her bed. She also made a pouch for the wheelchair, which she often used as she moved throughout the house. It held everything she needed—cordless phone, pen and pad, and her Kindle. Her crafts were on display throughout her house. It was like a museum, and there were always *oohs* and *ahhs* from everyone who came to visit.

I didn't like tedious crafts, just my writing, and I wanted my surroundings to enhance my ability to concentrate. I gave my bedroom/study the most considerations, as that's where I spent most of my time. I could be in there for days, researching and writing or just thinking. My desk had to conveniently house everything I needed— pens, pencils, highlighter, typing stand, lamp. Everything had to be within arm's length of my computer. There were two recliners; one I used at my desk, and one was for a guest. I had blackout curtains at my windows and window tint on each window pane. I loved the fall and spring and wanted to leave my windows up, but I was reluctant for security concerns. So I decided that if I attached screening to lattice and covered the entire window, I'd feel more secure. I'd had to call one of my old boyfriends, a handyman, to assist. For several days my friend and I worked on the project, and that's all I focused on until it was done. It was beautiful from the inside and out and served its intended purpose very well. When I couldn't get out, I could allow nature to flow in.

Baby-boy was also an artist who could lock himself away for days. He was always editing film, writing or doing research. He also spent lots of time learning to cook, so it wasn't unusual not to hear from him for days.

After he dropped me off, I did not hear from him for the entire weekend. When I took out the garbage on Monday morning, I noticed his car was gone. I assumed he'd gone to work. Around ten o'clock, as I watered my plants, I heard a key in the door. It was Baby-boy and he looked upset.

"What's wrong?" I asked.

"I'm not sure, but it looks like someone has been using my account," he said. "I'm going to the bank."

He hadn't been gone long when the phone rang; it was someone from the bank.

"Ms. Woodard, your son is here at the bank, and he's not feeling well. He asked me to call."

"I'm on my way."

When I got to the bank, they took me to one of the offices; he was just sitting there.

"Baby, what's wrong?" I asked.

"I don't know."

"Can you move?"

He stared straight ahead. "No, my heart feels like it's going to explode."

"Call an ambulance," I said to one of the employees.

When we got to the hospital, I was not allowed to stay with him while the doctors did their assessment. I waited frantically in the waiting area. I tried to call Tynisha because she was the closest to the hospital, and I needed someone there with me. She didn't answer, but I left a detailed message. Finally, they let me go to his room.

"What's wrong, baby?" I asked calmly.

"I don't know, Mama. I was signing some papers, and when I tried to stand up, my heart started beating so fast, and I got dizzy. They gave me some water, but it didn't stop. Now it feels like things are going in slow motion, like I'm not connected with the actual events. I can see everything happening, but there's a lag in time. Like if I try to touch you"—he reached out his hand—"it seems like you're far away."

"Calm down. Did you eat today?" I asked.

"No, I was going to eat something once I got to work. Then I got an email saying my bank account had been accessed. That's when I came home and stopped by your house. I don't know. I just feel strange, like I'm not in control. It's kind of like things are happening here"—he held up his left hand—"but I'm here"—he held up his right hand—"and all this space in between is not connected."

"You'll be fine," I replied. "Let's see what the doctor has to say. Just relax." I stood next to his bed, just rubbing his hand. I didn't mention it to him, but I noticed that his eyes seemed dull. They were no longer a vivid hazel. They were very light green and glossy.

I was trying to control my emotions. *Don't be shocked; don't be panicked. That's what the devil wants*, I told myself. For me, life was about good versus evil, God versus Satan. *The devil always wants to take your mind off Jesus. Pray, just pray.*

So I prayed: *Father, please, bind Satan's attack against my son. Father, please, in the name of Jesus. Please, God, protect my child. Cover him with the blood of the Lamb. Grace and mercy, Father!*

When Tynisha got there, I calmly gave her the latest information. I always tried to be strong, but as a mother, there was nothing worse than watching my child struggle.

He tried to explain to his sister, the disconnect he was experiencing. "It's so frustrating," he said. "I just want to scream. Maybe if I scream, I'll feel better."

"Bruh, don't scream; just calm down, and try to relax. Everything is going to be all right."

I found myself staring at him in total disbelief. I know my face showed my fright. I just had to walk out of the room. Once outside, I lost control of my emotions, and tears started to roll down my cheeks uncontrollably. I'd done well in most emergencies—Lord knows my kids had presented every challenge imaginable—but this was different, and I needed support, so I called my brother. He came immediately, and the sight of him made me so weak.

"What's wrong with him, sister?"

I was crying so hard I could not talk.

"Come on, sis; pull yourself together. It's going to be okay," he said as he hugged me.

Tynisha must have felt it was serious enough to call her best friend and spiritual confidant because suddenly there she was. She came over and just hugged me as my brother went inside.

"Let's just pray for a breakthrough," she said softly. "Father God, in the name of Jesus ..." she prayed.

When I got back to the room, the doctor was already there explaining his findings.

"Every test we did came back negative. Are you feeling stressed out about anything?"

"No," he replied, "just trying to get into grad school."

"I think you may have had a panic attack. It's not uncommon for a man your age. The EKG—the test that measures the electrical activity of the heartbeat—is a little abnormal, so I recommend you follow up with your regular doctor and have him look at it. I'm going to prescribe a mild sedative and write you off work for a few days. If this continues, I want you to come back to the emergency room."

For the next few days he slept a lot, but when he was awake, he still tried to understand and explain the disconnect he felt at the bank. He was different than my other children. By age eighteen, all three of my other children and I—as well as most people I knew—had already made decisions that would affect their lives forever. Even though Baby-boy had lost his father at age seven, on the surface, he was an average kid. He completed high school by age seventeen and college by twenty-one. Most people in the neighborhood looked up to him as a role model. His pants didn't sag, he didn't smoke or drink alcohol, and, perhaps most noticeably, he did not use slang. Listening to him speak made me wonder how he could live around people who used improper English, even his mother, on a regular basis and not allow it to rub off on him.

Most people would probably view his issues as tiny compared to many. He didn't have kids, wasn't in trouble with the law, and had a decent job. They couldn't fathom how not getting into graduate school could cause this much frustration. He, on the other hand, could not understand why people made decisions that could cost them their livelihoods. Nonetheless, regardless of the viewpoint, everyone needed to identify and overcome their obstacles as they pursued their goals. If not, they will get "caught in the web." The issues they face can negatively impact their entire lives, if they aren't handled properly.

In times like these, I leaned more toward my faith because I knew the devil was always busy spinning that web. He was the author of confusion, and his preventing us from achieving our full God-given potential was his only purpose.

Over the next few weeks, Baby-boy seemed to be okay, but was he really? What triggered a panic attack? What was going on in his head? I asked what was on his mind, and he responded with one word: "Nothing." I didn't push, but from time to time I'd ask again, and every time I did, he gave the same one-word answer. I continued to pray, trust God and show my baby as much love as I possibly could. I also tried to make him understand that whether it was a painful past, or someone treating us unfairly, or a decision we made, everything had the potential to become webs that hinder our success.

"Our goal in life should be to reach our greatest potential," I told him gently. "We should strive to be the best we can be. I know the limits webs can put on us if we do not break free. I stayed caught up for years. Question after question clouded my mind—How could they? Why did he?—and mentally, I could not move on. I could not focus on my future because I was stuck on the past. But do you know what helped?" I waited for him to respond, but when he didn't, I took a deep breath and continued. "I learned to talk to God. Instead of just thinking, I asked God the questions. *How could they treat me so unfairly, Father? Father, why must I suffer for the bad things done to me.* Every question I had, every emotion I felt, I told my Father in heaven. *They hurt me Father, but I know according to your words, I must forgive. I must let it go so I can move on.* Then and only then, through my relationship with the Lord, did I began to find peace—not answers, but peace."

"Mother, that's your faith. I don't have that. I mean, I try to pray. I want to have that kind of faith, but I don't think God hears me."

"Baby, God hears you, and he know you better than you know yourself. The Bible says if you have the faith of a mustard seed, nothing will be impossible for you. I want you to develop a stronger relationship with God. You must learn to trust him with every decision." I took him in the room and closed the door. "Let's talk about prayer. In the Bible, Jesus says you shall not be as the hypocrites who love to pray, standing in the synagogues and in the corners of the streets, that they may be seen of men. But when you pray, enter into your room, and when you have shut your door, pray to your Father in secret, and your Father who sees in secret shall reward you openly. If you don't know what to pray about, pray like Jesus directed. Come on, let me show you."

We got down on our knees together, and I prayed.

"Our Father who art in heaven, hallowed be thy name. Thy kingdom come. Thy will be done, on earth as it is in heaven. Give us this day our daily bread, and forgive our debts as we forgive our debtors. Lead us not into temptation, but deliver us from evil, for thine is the kingdom and the power and the glory forever. Amen."

Day by day, we continued to talk about the importance of having God in our lives. Baby-boy opened-up more and more. I began to see and understand his issues and frustration. He had faced many challenges for such a young man. He'd lost his father at an early age. He had to give up sports after his leg injury. He broke up with his girlfriend, as many young men do. Still, the biggest issue was his ambition. He was an artist, and for a true artist, life has a different drive. A true artist doesn't just go to work and back but works all the time in his mind until he breaks through in what his talent is. That was the case with my baby boy. He loved film production. That was his passion—not just shooting footage but putting movies together.

I can remember when I came home, and there was a crowd of people at my house. Most of them were white, and they stood out like a sore thumb in my neighborhood. It turned out that they'd been filming but they needed a new location, so he brought them home to finish the shoot. Watching him direct was captivating. I watched his every move, trying to understand as he was guiding and directing the entire group. Then when the main character didn't show up, he had to get Dewayne to play the sheriff. Dewayne was very theatrical, and they worked together well in a short time and pulled it all together. We sat there watching a short film produced by Baby-boy and Dewayne became the star.

There was a fire raging inside my baby boy, and he needed a breakthrough. He needed God to put his work in the hands of the right people at the right time. He needed God to bind Satan's attacks against him and allow his gift from his heavenly Father to shine through. I prayed and asked God to help him find his way. I trusted God, and I had learned to just say, "Thank you. All is well."

Many months passed and could tell that Baby-boy was maturing spiritually. I encouraged him to listen to Joel Osteen. Many mornings I would listen to Joel's message and notice a direct correlation to something we were going through. Finally, I noticed some major changes. There was no longer his sense of urgency. He expressed other paths he could take towards accomplishing his dreams. Oh, it was painful to see him going through this process, but I knew he was going to be a better man in God's time.

I knew my children had to develop a strong relationship with God, and they did. Whether it was issues they faced being young mothers or they were in trouble, sick, or some other thing, hearing them say they were praying about it gave me peace.

Baby-boy however, was still young in his faith, and this was harder for him. I continued to guide him the best way I knew. I told him the importance of having a personal relationship with God. I taught him how to pray and read the Bible. But until he learned to trust God no matter what, issues would always seem extreme.

It hurt my heart to see young people struggling to find their way in life. I knew the feeling they carried around with them—always in deep thought, trying to figure out that perfect move, word, or action that would help propel their lives to the next level. I understood how these issues could easily cause anxiety, which might lead to panic attacks. My baby boy had to learn that regardless of his struggles or success, peace come from the Lord. Real joy comes from the love of God.

11

Mentoring is a Gift from God

Mentoring has always come natural for me. I always felt like I had a responsibility to train young people, and for as long as I can remember, time after time, I've been afforded that opportunity. As a young mother, I would take my kids to the park. Often it wasn't just my three but several others from the neighborhood as well. *You hold his hand, and I'll hold her hand. Wait. Now walk quickly; don't run.* When my children got older, their teenage friends were constantly at our home. I cooked, fed, counseled, and cared for them as if they were my own. Then, as a drill sergeant, I trained young people to become soldiers. Still, I was totally surprised by my ability to manage children with special needs. I was afraid of their behavior because of my experience with a special-needs boy I'd met when I was growing up.

Ray-Ray was the teenage son of the lady who did my hair. She was a friend of Mama's, and they lived a few blocks away, so Mama would send me there alone. When I got there, this kid would be slobbering and making strange noises and gestures. He always tried to kiss me. His mama would say, "Stop Ray-Ray," over and over, but he would not leave me alone.

"He won't hurt you," she'd say. "He just loves himself some Karah. He gets so excited when you come around."

I was terrified until I left there. As an adult I learned more about disabilities and was no longer fearful, but honestly, I was still a bit leery when I was around people with special needs. After I retired from the military and finished college, I applied for a job as a substitute teacher. I wanted to ease back into the workforce. Again, my ability to effectively work with children was noted. I only assisted at one school but worked in different classrooms, so most of the students were familiar with me. Then one day, as soon as the principal opened the door to my assigned room, I knew there was going to be a problem. These were children with special needs, and they were acting out. *Oh, my God, please Father*, I prayed. *I am going to need an anointing today.*

The principal introduced me to the class and then quietly explained their needs to me. I felt frozen for a few minutes, but I began to relax a little. Then she said to the class, "Y'all be good for Ms. Woodard," and she whispered to me, "I'll be back to check on you in a little while."

"Be good," I thought. *Do these kids even know what that means?*

One round-faced black boy held a pencil and was moving it back and forth between his fingers as he walked around the room with his head tilted to the left. His gaze toward the ceiling prompted me to look, but I saw nothing there. His appearance, however, captured my attention. His jeans were pressed with a crease down each leg. His red-and-white plaid shirt was tucked in, and his belt matched his black-leather sneakers.

"Sit down, y'all," said a slim black kid in a wheelchair, his voice trembling. "Sit down."

I was dumbfounded as to how I would handle these children. Suddenly, I thought about music. Kids liked music, and I knew many children's songs. So I sang, and they started to calm down. The ones who could join in soon sang along with me. It was September, but at one point we sang "We Wish You a Merry Christmas" because that's all I could think of. I didn't teach much that day, but I often was called back to that classroom as a teacher's aide, and that allowed me the opportunity to work closer and get more comfortable with the children.

Finally, I'd found a method that worked with each of them, and I became a valued part of the staff. I was regularly called over the loudspeaker to come to that room to assist. At the end of the school year, the principal offered me a regular position as a classroom aide, and I accepted. To my total amazement, I was now the go-to person for properly handling special-needs children. I was employed at the school for two full terms. Then, at the beginning of the third term, someone told me of a job that might be even more rewarding.

There was an opening for a food service supervisor at a large hospital, and I wanted to check it out. After all, that was my specialty and although I never thought I would work in food services again after the military, hospital food service was a little different and deserved my consideration. I went in for a walk through of the facility and was introduced to some of the employees.

One girl walked up and said, "Hi, my name is Emily. I clean the tables. What's your name?"

"Karah," I replied. "Nice to meet you, Emily."

"I like you. Are you going to be my new boss?"

The manager stepped in then, saying, "Okay, Emily, enough questions for now. You have a lot of work to do."

"Oh, okay," she said as she grabbed her bucket of water.

The manager explained to me that Emily was an employee with special needs and had been working there for five years.

I thought about Ray-Ray and the special-needs classroom. God was certainly preparing me for something. I took the job and worked with Emily and twenty-five other food service employees for the next seven years. During that time, I saw every personality and every problem imaginable. Even so, I enjoyed every experience and consider that one of my most rewarding jobs.

Based on my previous experience and the fact that I have four adult children, ten grandchildren, and one great-grandchild, it is clear to me that God placed me in a position of influence in the lives of many of his children. That is a blessing. His grace has allowed me to be a positive influence in the lives of many young people. I have dedicated much of my life to mentoring, and while I cannot say with certainty how effective I was, I'm proud that I did so with pure love and good intentions.

My philosophy on mentoring is, "If you can't help them, at least don't hurt them." These are God's children, and I believe if you lead them astray, God will hold you accountable. Satan, however, is a fierce enemy. He will do everything he can to take your attention off the Lord. Our young people are often powerless prey for Satan to attack. I've witnessed a lack of guidance and patience from those who should be mentoring children and young adults, and that's hard for me to accept. These adults seem to forget the days of their youth. They act as though they were never young and never made mistakes or bad decisions. Most egregious are the adults who take advantage of children or contribute to their delinquency. If I were a politician, this would be my platform. I would make this a violation of the law and send the strongest message possible to those who violate it—"Leave our young people alone. Allow them to grow up without your influencing them in the wrong direction." There could only be selfish reasons for adults who rob children of their innocence, and that is inexcusable.

As a Christian, spiritual guidance has become the most important mentoring I can provide. I am no Bible scholar and cannot reference many Bible verses from memory; my personal experience with God, however, speaks volumes, and that's what I usually refer to. Whenever the opportunity presents itself, I am eager to talk about my Father in heaven. I try not to be overbearing, but if I'm asked how or why I'd chose a particular path in my life or how I survived injustices, unfairness, or even lack of courage, I always talk about my relationship with God.

Whether it was my Father from heaven speaking to me as a young girl or an angel in the image of my brother during Desert Storm, I've always known it was God providing guidance and strength through whatever means necessary. Then, when he speaks directly to my spirit, as he did when my husband was diagnosed with cancer, it leaves no doubt. *"I knew when I joined you two together that this day would come."* I heard it—or should I say I felt it. It was a special kind of communication that shattered all doubts.

For me to be effective in my guidance and in my own resistance to attacks of evil, quick assessments are required. I've learned to close my mouth and pray. There have been too many times when a person's behavior has left me in shock. Quickly, my eyes and mouth would open wide, and I'd spend too much time wondering how a person could behave in that way. Fortunately, I'm no longer as shocked by people's behavior because I know that the devil is busy; therefore, evil is always lurking. I now view my shock as a trick of the devil. His goal is to take my mind off God, to bombard me with questions and confusion so I lose focus from God's guidance. Some behaviors simply defy understanding. Therefore, the more I stay connected or the quicker I reconnect to God after such instances, the simpler life will be.

I am honored that God has trusted me with the care of so many of his children. I am forever grateful for the presence of God through the Holy Spirit, which guides and protects me.

I want the God in me to shine as bright as a beacon as I continue my journey through life. As I fall on my knees, I plead for grace and mercy for all youths.

Father, please, in the name of Jesus, have mercy on our children. Cover them with your grace, and guide them through the Holy Spirit. Help them to find their way to you, Father. Help them to know that you are God, and keep them strong against Satan's attacks. Father, please, keep us in your grace and mercy. Thank you, Father, for these blessings. In the name of your Son, Jesus Christ. Amen.

12

In Pursuit of a Dream

From the time I tore blank pages out of old books so I could have writing paper, I knew I had to write. I wrote out of anger and pain most of the time, but writing was always important to me. I didn't think about becoming a literary expert. In fact, I never did much reading. I preferred to spend my time in writing. I would keep paper and pencils handy. I would ask for typing paper while waiting at the doctor's office or for other appointments.

When I joined the military, I was always required to have a pen and memo pad. Normally, mine was filled with scribbling and my attempts at short stories. I tried to write from many awkward places. After lights-out was called, I used a flashlight underneath the covers. I tried to write from the back of a truck while surrounded by equipment. On boats and airplanes, I whipped out my paper and pen and tried to write. No matter what was going on around me, I found the need to write, even in the desert during war.

Then, when I went back to college, I was required to organize and make time for my writing. Eventually, I was given a column in the school newspaper. It felt great, and my desire to write more often intensified. Life was still raging out of control, and staying focused was not easy.

When I attempted to write my first book, *Vengeance Is Mine: the Key to Peace and Freedom from Injustices,* I had many doubts. I wasn't sure why or if I should spend my time trying to write a book. So I simply asked God, "Father, is this your will, or am I just wasting my time?" Immediately, I heard, *"To tell your story is to tell my story. It is time for us to take a bow."* God had given me his blessing. From that point, I was focused primarily on becoming an author. I could hear Mama saying, *"Go live your life. Your children are grown. They will find their way."*

Day after day, however, I found it harder and harder to concentrate. There was too much going on around me. My neighborhood was too busy. Whenever I tried to write, my thoughts were interrupted. I could hear car doors slamming, children yelling, music playing. That propelled me to finalize a decision I'd pondered for years—I had to move. I had to find a place where my creative juices flowed freely.

I'd always loved Hawaii. The beaches and the sunshine lifted my spirits and opened my mind. After my last trip there, however, I knew Hawaii wasn't my destination of choice. It was simply too far away. The long flight was too uncomfortable, and I needed to live closer to my children. I started thinking about Florida and could not get it out of my mind. It had everything I wanted—sunshine, beaches, military bases—and it was not too far from home. Yes, Florida sounded like the perfect place for me. I was excited about the idea of moving, but where in Florida should I live? It was time to explore, so I called my friend Lawrence, who had been born and raised there but settled in Savannah, Georgia, after he got out of the military.

Lawrence and I were stationed together in Hawaii and stayed in contact over the years. I told him about my plans and asked him to accompany me, and he was eager to go. We both had SUVs and felt that gas would be too expensive for this exploration. So I decided to rent a more economical and fun vehicle. I drove to Savannah to pick up Lawrence. I pulled up to his house in a red Volkswagen GTI convertible and just started tooting the horn.

Oh, my goodness, I thought as I saw him for the first time in ten years. "Wow, you've picked up a few pounds since the last time I saw you!"—the words just flew out of my mouth.

"Yeah, more of me to love," he replied. "Come here, girl, and give me a hug."

I did, but his hug was a little too strong, and his comments were more inappropriate than the ones that flew from my mouth. "OK, let me go now, and don't you start," I said.

Lawrence always had expressed interest in me, but there was just no chemistry. I once had considered dating him, but there had to be chemistry, and I felt none. I had made that very clear to him in the past, but that did not stop his flirtatious comments and sexual innuendos.

This is going to be a long trip, I thought.

"Come on in," he said, "while I make sure everything is locked up. The characters around here are always lurking. I might not have much, but they might have even less."

Yes, sir, I thought, *you need to upgrade this furniture*. There was nothing modern anywhere. Everything looked drab and worn. I guess it was comfortable for him, but no woman would feel comfortable in this bachelor pad, especially not me.

I opened the trunk to put his bags in, and that started an ongoing conversation about the size of the car.

"Girl, this is a small car. I might not even fit in this thing. You know I got long legs."

"Oh, hush, you'll be fine. Just let the seat go all the way back," I replied.

Jacksonville was less than an hour away, so we stopped there for lunch. I knew that was not where I wanted to be. Geographically, I wanted to be somewhere between Orlando and Miami. I had done some research online and learned a lot about both cities. I knew these cities had everything to which I wanted regular access. In addition to the theme parks, college campuses, and nightlife, they each had a large military retirement community and treatment facilities. Still, I had no desire to live in either place. I knew I would not like the traffic and noise of a big city. I needed a quaint little area in between the two. I wasn't sure where, but I was certain I would know it when I saw it.

We arrived in Orlando later that afternoon and, following Lawrence's directions, found a nice hotel in the downtown area. I wanted to relax and map out some areas to explore around the city. The hotel looked exquisite, I could tell it would be costly. But it was in the best location so we decided to stay. Once inside I marveled at the design. It was as if the hotel was turned outside in. The skylight allowed natural light to engulf the entire area. The hallways on each floor made a complete circle, allowing direct entry to each room.

"Good afternoon," said the man behind the counter. "May I help you?"

"Yes, we need a room," Lawrence quickly replied.

"Single or double?" the attendant asked.

"Single," Lawrence replied.

"No," I interjected, "double."

"Double?" the attendant repeated.

"Yes, double," I said as I glared at Lawrence.

"Two single beds," the attendant replied as he gave us each a key. We headed to the elevator.

"Oh, it's like that?" Lawrence asked.

"Like what?"

"We could have slept in the same bed," he said. "I wouldn't touch you if you didn't want me to."

"Let's not go there, Lawrence. We can share a room—there is nothing wrong with that—but we are not sleeping together."

"Man, you be tripping, as long as I have been wanting you."

When we got to our room on the fourth floor, I looked down at the beautiful atrium. The mahogany reception desk was a magnificent work of art. Tiny leaves etched onto branches filled the entire wall like a towering tree. Someone had put a lot of hours into that. I looked around the room. The waterfalls on the opposite wall provided a soothing sound as the water flowed gradually onto the rocks below. A mahogany bar was in the center of the room, with mahogany lounge chairs throughout, all with leaves carved in detail. People sipped on cocktails, as if they were lounging around a swimming pool.

"Oh, this is nice," I said as we walked into the room.

"Yeah, whatever," he replied.

"Which bed do you prefer?" I asked as I walked toward the window.

"The same one you are sleeping in."

"Lawrence, we are not sleeping in the same bed. Now which one?"

"The one closest to the bathroom, then, because I might have to take a few cold showers tonight."

I shook my head. "Oh, my God."

To our surprise, the window opened out onto a private balcony, and the view was sensational. The room was so amazing that I quickly forgot the $140 it cost per night.

We sat and talked as I searched different areas on my smartphone, but I soon realized it did not reveal enough detail.

"Hey, I need a full-sized map. I'm going to that auto store across the street to see if they have one."

"I'll go with you," Lawrence said. "Don't start walking around here alone. People will try to take advantage."

We went to get the map, and along the way, I noticed how friendly the people were. This was a tourist town, and many of the passersby no doubt were on vacation, which makes a huge difference in attitude. We spent the evening exploring the map. I would pick out a place that fit my preference of location. He'd comment on what he knew or didn't know about the area. We finally decided on a place called Sebring. I liked it because it was about midway between Orlando, Tampa, and Miami. Also, while I loved the water, weather from the surrounding ocean was unpredictable, so I did not want to be too close. Sebring was between Florida's east and west coasts, but it had several lakes nearby, which was perfect. I was excited. I researched everything I could about Sebring and the surrounding area, and I fell asleep with the map and phone.

I woke up the next morning and walked out on the balcony. My world was changed forever; this place was spectacular. I stood there, scanning the area, searching for anything I could identify. Shopping centers, parks, lakes, highways, buses, trolleys, and people kept me intrigued for a while.

Lawrence grumbled, "Hey, boo, you ready to get our day started?"

"Well, I was just thinking …" I said as I turned to look at him. "Could we stay here one more night? I think I'd like to check out this area more?"

"Sure," he replied, "there is a lot to see in this area. But I thought you wanted to be away from the city."

"Yeah, I thought so too, but this city might not be so bad. Let's just check it out before we go any farther.

"Fine with me," he replied.

"Let me take a quick shower."

"Hey, take your time, and if you want me to, I can wash your back."

"Oh, how sweet, but I think I can manage."

"Well, you can't blame a man for trying."

We each showered and dressed as we talked about the area.

"I don't work, so traffic is not an issue for me," I said. "If I could find a quiet studio apartment that I could afford, this area would be just fine."

"Now, that may be an issue. I'm not sure about the cost of an apartment in this area. Could be expensive."

"Well, let's have breakfast here at the hotel and then walk a few miles and see as much as we can."

"Sounds like a plan."

Lawrence was totally unfamiliar with downtown Orlando. He said he had been there many times but always had his children with him and went directly to a specific theme park.

Before we left the hotel, I asked the clerk if there was a street that would take us around the city.

"Yes, right out here is Biscayne Avenue, which basically circles downtown Orlando. You can take a left or right on Biscayne, and it will eventually bring you right back to the hotel." He smiled and added, "Remember, though, I said *eventually*. It's about eight or ten miles. But you can always cut through downtown to get back here."

"I'm wearing my best walking shoes, and my cell phone has GPS," I said. "I'm sure we'll be fine."

We had not walked a block before we started pointing out places of interest. Beautiful churches and cathedrals were on almost every corner, much like downtown in my city. There were also just as many nightclubs, pubs, and lounges. There was a huge transit station with buses and trolleys within a few blocks.

"Oh, there's the Orange County library," I said excitedly. "Oh yes, this is nice—very convenient."

"That excited you? The library?"

"Of course," I said. "I plan on doing lots of reading and writing in the future, so access to a library is important."

"There's the courthouse ... and the jail," he said with a smirk, and we both laughed. "Yep, they can save a lot of gas transporting the guilty—just walk them right next door."

"Wow," I exclaimed, "there's the lake we saw from the balcony. Let's grab something to drink from one of these stores. We can take a break when we get to the lake."

WELCOME TO LAKE EOLA PARK, the sign read. I could see to the other side, but this was a huge lake. Ducks and geese floated on the water, making the only noise that could be heard. The area around it was immaculate. Not a thing appeared out of place. The grass was well manicured, and hedges were trimmed neatly. Sidewalks and benches were situated throughout the area, though some benches were uncomfortably close to the water. The sign reminding pet owners to pick up their poop made me think of Naomi and her doggies. I couldn't help but smile.

"What's so funny?" Lawrence asked.

I gave him a clear picture of Naomi and her basset hounds. Then I told him that she cleaned their butts with baby wipes when they returned from their walks, and he could not believe it. I shared a few more stories about Naomi and the dogs before we decided to move on. We were both getting too relaxed and didn't know how much farther it was to the hotel.

Soon we came upon the performing arts center, and my enthusiasm reached its highest point. "Oh, my goodness, I cannot believe this." I stopped directly in front of the sign and read, "'Dr. Phillips Performing Arts Center.' This is perfect. I have everything I need right here within walking distance. I would go to all the musicals and stage plays. Oh, my God, I think this is it. This might be my new home."

"You are serious, aren't you?"

"Most definitely very serious. I need to be inspired and entertained, and this place has it all. Plus, I'm not too far from home if I need to get there in a hurry. I can drive or take a flight. I don't even need a car;

there appears to be a large transit system. Plus, everything is within walking distance, which is unbelievable."

"There are the Cobb movie theaters and the Amtrak station," Lawrence said.

"Oh, wait—you have to be kidding me," I said as I noticed a sign.

"What?"

"Is that what I think it is?"

"Where? What?"

"Right next to the Amtrak station—are those apartments?"

"It sure looks like it—55 West Apartments. Let's go check it out."

The sign indicated there were one-, two- and three-bedroom apartments available. The price range was $650 to $1,500 per month. My mouth flew open, and I stared at Lawrence.

"Now, that's reasonable," he said.

We couldn't see much from where we stood. The view was obscured by shrubbery and brick walls on each side of the entrance. We didn't venture onto the property. The sign and location provided enough details at the time.

"Let me slow down," I said. I took a deep breath and exhaled slowly. "I don't want to get too excited and start drawing conclusions."

We walked and talked, but this little downtown area continued to amaze me. The German restaurant and cobblestone road took me back to my days in Kitzingen and Wurzburg, Germany. My love affair with K. C. came to mind, and as I daydreamed, I didn't see or hear anything else along the way. Soon we were back at the hotel, and my mind was all over the place. We spent the night enjoying all the amenities of the hotel. The hotel alone was reason enough to come back. It had many dining rooms, a piano bar, great food, a sauna and Jacuzzi, several pools, and a full exercise room. Still, I cherished the terrace the most. It provided a view of my new favorite place, and I relished the possibilities.

13

Breakthrough

After my road trip I started thinking through the options of making the move. Everything was coming together. My doctors had finally prescribed medications to manage most of my issues. It was up to me to do my part. I felt exhausted all the time, so no matter what I was doing, I had to rest a lot. Stress had to be minimized, as did many of my regular activities. While I was adjusting very well medically, I still had an uneasy feeling. Nevertheless, I continued with the planning. I made the process final by renting a one-bedroom apartment in downtown Orlando. It was a small apartment, but it had a balcony and security, and that was enough to finalize my decision. I would drive there and stay for short periods, but I couldn't stop thinking about the children. Despite the fact they were all grown, and I was within driving distance, leaving again created anxiety. Mothers who left the family were unusual in my community, and I had already left once. That time it was for business, and despite the negative consequences, the benefits were far greater. This time, however, it was simply my preference.

The children were excited about the move, mainly about the nearby beaches and theme parks. They immediately begin discussing their first trip to visit me. My baby boy, however, appeared less enthused. His own issues overshadowed his emotions. He often expressed anger, frustration, or just lack of understanding toward many things. I knew it had begun with the loss of his father—prior to that, he was an engaging kid who kept everyone entertained—but while that was understandable, his mind-set obstructed his vision for his own future. His glass was always half empty with regard to life in general. Despite all I'd gone through in life, mine glass was always half full. His pessimistic comments, wrapped in acerbic humor, kept me wondering what he was thinking. I needed to help him change his perspective on life, so we talked.

Unfortunately, my other children and I didn't confer much about life decisions. Usually, we just made our decisions and accepted the consequences. For me, there was one major exception—my decision to join the military. Mama had been a major part in making that happen, so we had worked together to reach that decision. Other than that, I just talked to God.

Baby boy was different; he enjoyed our conversations. He liked to talk and share most of the time, but sometimes he got overwhelmed and became frustrated. Still, we talked primarily about good versus evil and the importance of developing a personal relationship with God. We also talked about his career goals.

"What's your dream, your goal in life?" I asked.

"I want to see my films on the big screen."

I was excited that he could identify exactly what he wanted in life. Still, I had to make sure he was prepared if things didn't manifest according to his plans. "That's wonderful," I said. "Just remember that God know what's best for us, and ultimately it's his will that will be done. When our dreams and goals come into agreement with his plan for our lives, that's when major breakthroughs happen."

I told him about my dream as a young girl and how long I'd been working toward that dream. "Even though we can't always see things progressing in that direction," I told him, "it doesn't mean it's not happening. As I look back over my life, I can see that God was ordering my steps. I was focused primarily on heartache and pain, but God was focused on everything. Now I can see the manifestation of his plan. I hope that one day you'll look back and see the same with your life, but for now, you just must trust and believe. Remember that in the natural, things may seem impossible, but God works in the supernatural, and he can bless your dream in the blink of an eye. So never give up. Just keep enjoying your life, keep the dream alive, and trust that God will put you on the path he wants you to go."

All my children and several of my adult grandchildren were trying to find their way. Some were adventurous; others were stubborn, even reckless, at times. The paths they took often led to trouble and hardships. Nevertheless, they knew the Lord, and as they continued to grow, I hoped their woes would become experiences that influenced a different thought process. That's what had happened to me, and I shared those experiences. Everyone thought my children would make my life hard and my goals unattainable. That may have been true to a certain extent, but they also fueled my determination. Now, as adults, they had to make their own decisions. I continued to pray for them, and by the grace of God, they would find their way.

Many young people make decisions at an early age that will change their lives forever. I knew many girls who had babies, young boys who were incarcerated, and both girls and boys who became addicted to drugs before they were twenty-one. That concerned me, so I continued to pray, and I urged children to pray.

I always had the hardest time trusting anyone with my children, even God. I remember being consumed with what to do to help them grow up to become responsible adults. Their behavior was out of control, and I had no peace. Then God spoke the following words into my spirit: *"As long as you are running to their rescue, they never will learn to trust in me."* That immediately changed my perspective.

One day, as I was about to leave for Florida for the weekend, Baby-boy came in and he was in a great mood.

"Well, Mama," he said with a big grin, "I may not be here when you get back. I got a promising job offer in New Jersey. I talked with Grandma, and she said I could live there with her if I like."

His paternal grandmother lived in New Jersey and so did most of his dad's family. He would be surrounded by family, and hopefully that would take some pressure off both of us. This was the most exciting news he'd had in a very long time.

"I'm so happy for you! I knew everything would come together in God's time."

There is nothing more important to me than knowing that my children are finding their way. Their relationship with God is a key component in the pursuit of their happiness. Once baby boy developed a close relationship with God, we each could pursue our dreams—peacefully.

14

Cinderella Has No Curfew

It took a lot of courage for me to make the final move to this vibrant new city, but each time I went to Orlando, I instantly became a brand-new me. Downtown Orlando gave me everything I needed and much more. I moved into a nice apartment with a view. I couldn't see the ocean, but I could see several lakes, including the ducks in Lake Eola Park. I bought a small SUV, but I didn't need it often.

Life was beautiful, and I tried to enjoy every moment. Initially, I spent most of my time alone. I was writing feverishly to finish the novel I was working on. Most evenings I'd take my bubble bath, lavish myself with lotion, and put on my lounge wear and perfume as if I was expecting a date. I'd turn on my music, pour a glass of wine, and relax for the night.

Finally, after months of lying dormant, my revisions were complete. I sent the book back to the editor and made plans to go out and celebrate. After going through my bubble-bath, lotion, and makeup ritual, I slipped into a short, sexy polka-dot sundress and strappy sandals. I fingered through my wrapped hair and went out the door. It was Thursday, and the jazz lounge a few doors down was calling my name.

I walked through the door, confident, with a gentle smile. I had to smile to disguise what my granddaughters called "resting witch face."

Although it was my natural facial expression, I had to focus hard on not looking angry. The sexy young bartender made things much easier when he cheerfully introduced himself.

"My name is Nazzorie, and I am your friendly bartender."

Now I had a reason to release my true gift—a smile that lit up the room. "Hi, Nazzorie," I responded. "I'm Karah. Do you have a nickname?"

"You may hear some people call me Nazz, but I hate that."

"Why?"

"Because when they get full of liquor and call me *Nazz*, it sounds like they are calling me *ass*."

"Oh no!" I said, and we laughed a long hearty laugh. "Whew, that was funny. I needed that laugh."

Nazzorie nodded. "What can I get for you, Karah?"

"Can you fix me something with gin? I'll try whatever you suggest."

"If you like the taste of gin, I can sexy it up a bit. I'll be right back." He returned with a the long, slender frosted glass, moist from the ice.

"Now that is pretty," I said.

"This, my dear, is a French 75; it is simply gin, lemon juice, and champagne and a bit of nectar."

"Nice," I replied and took a few sips. "Very nice. Thank you, Nazzorie."

"My pleasure."

"Hey, Nazz!" someone yelled.

I laughed as he rolled his eyes and then winked at me. "I'll be back to check on you, Ms. Karah."

I continued to enjoy the evening, listening to the music and having a few drinks. Soon, I needed to go to the restroom. On my way, I noticed that the place was getting busy. On my way back to the bar, someone grabbed me by the hand.

"Excuse me. My name is Ted—Theodore Hamilton. I noticed you sitting alone. Would you mind if I joined you?"

"Hi, Ted. My name is Karah. If this is your table, maybe I should join you. I plan to have another drink, and that bar stool may become risky."

"Yes, of course join me, and allow me to buy you a drink. What are you having?"

I had to think for a second. "French 75."

"Hm, sounds dangerous. I've never heard of that." He got Nazzorie's attention, pointed to me, and gestured *two*. "I think I'll have one with you. I've only had a couple of beers."

Nazzorie brought the drinks over as Ted and I became acquainted. I waited for him to take his first sip. As soon as he did, he started smacking his lips together to accentuate the taste.

"How do you like it?" I asked.

"Needs more liquor, for sure," he said and then grinned. "No, it's fine. I like it, and I like you." He held up his glass; I followed. "To new beginnings."

"To new beginnings," I echoed.

Ted and I talked for hours. He was an insurance adjuster from Jacksonville. He'd come down to Orlando for some gambling and nightlife. He explained that he had been there a week and only had two days left. He asked me to dinner for the following evening, and I agreed.

I dressed to impress every time I walked out the door, and dinner with Ted was no different. My skinny black dress was almost too skinny. I could hear my children and grandchildren saying, "Now wait a minute, Ms. Woodard. Where are you going with that tight dress on?" I laughed to myself and strutted right on out the door.

Ted knew a place a few blocks away called Spice Steakhouse. It was only a ten-minute pleasurable walk, even in heels. That was one benefit of this town—no need to get in a car with a stranger for a date. We enjoyed each other's company—I liked Ted, and he liked me—and I hated to see him leave the next day. We exchanged contact information and said our goodbyes. The next day, after my walk, I found a note on my apartment door: "See front desk attendant immediately." I went back down to the desk and asked about the note.

"Oh, Ms. Woodard, you have a package. Just a second." She returned with yellow roses in a crystal vase. The vase had something etched in black—it was a large heart, with "French 75" and "Spice" centered in the heart. There also was a card that read, "Just so you will remember me. Thank you, Karah. You are the best."

This was the beginning of the life I'd dreamed of for years. Eventually, I had a social life that was filled with excitement, and my social calendar was overflowing. I met many new people, including some retirees who were extremely nice and liked to dance. I was still very youthful, and my dance skills were significantly better than theirs, but they were eager, and I never said no. They also provided information on the best deals around the area.

One day I was at one of the activity centers when I heard a younger woman talking about roller skating, and I had to go over and introduce myself.

"Hi, my name is Karah. Did I hear you mention roller skating?"

"Yes, ma'am, you sure did. My name is Emily, and I work at Astro Skating Center."

"I just moved here, and I love skating rinks. How far is it?"

"It's about a fifteen-minute walk from here."

"I'll have to check it out. I'm not what I used to be on skates, but I can still go slow."

"You go, girl. As I said, I work at Astro, but there are several skate centers in this area."

"Great. I'll look them up. I haven't ventured too far from downtown yet, but I will now. I would love to go, even just to watch the other skaters."

"Maybe I'll see you there."

"Yes, Emily. Nice meeting you."

"Likewise, Karah."

It had been only three months since I'd moved to Orlando, and I had found my peace. I had my favorite club, fitness center, walking route, and church. My schedule was full, and I hadn't yet driven my car. Lawrence wanted to come down for the weekend to see how I was settling in, and he wanted to bring a girl with him.

That seemed curious, but I said, "Yes, bring her. Y'all come on. I'll sleep on the couch and give you two the bedroom." If Lawrence had a woman in his life, I was going to help them make it. He was worse than I was with regard to dating. I had never met any of his girlfriends and never heard him speak of any. With his new girl, surely he had lost interest in me.

I went grocery shopping and got everything ready for their visit. I didn't make any plans; I decided to wait so we could discuss it together.

Late Friday evening, they arrived at the apartment. I went down to add them to the visitors log; then they could come and go without me.

"Hi, Lawrence, glad you made it."

"Karah, this is Cecilia."

"It's a pleasure to meet you, Cecilia," I said as I reached for her hand.

"It's a pleasure to meet you, Karah," she said, giving my hand an affectionate squeeze.

I noticed her thick foreign accent immediately, but I couldn't place it.

"Lawrence has told me so much about you, Karah. You and I are going to be sisters."

"Great. That will be an honor," I responded.

On the way up to my apartment, Cecilia said, "Karah, I am from Haiti, and sometimes my speech is not very clear. You just tell me, 'Girl, slow down. I don't know what you are saying.' That is what Lawrence tells me all the time."

We all laughed. She didn't look Haitian; she looked more Latino. Her skin was dark brown and smooth, and her hair was short and curly. This girl was a breath of fresh air, and I couldn't help but wonder how these two got together.

Once in my place, we put the bags away, and I asked what they would like to do. I was thinking about the next day, but Cecilia had a different idea in mind.

"It is Friday night. Let's go party. Karah, you like to party, yes?"

"Of course," I replied.

"Lawrence, sweetie, Karah and I want to go dancing. You take us, baby?"

"That's up to y'all; we can go wherever you want to go, honey."

"Karah, you know a good party place?"

"Well, there are several clubs in the area. I usually go to a jazz club up the street."

"No, no jazz. Bahamian, reggae, something with a beat so I can dance my way."

I was a bit shocked by her comments, but she was entertaining, to say the least. "Let me search the web and see where the nearest reggae club is," I said. "Looks like there's one over by the art center, which is only a few blocks away. But I don't know anything about it. It might be boring."

"Girl, it will not be boring when we get there, I will show them how to have a good time. Karah, girl, you need flat shoes, baby. I warn you. Maybe we will be barefoot before the night is over."

We made the short walk to the club following the GPS, and when we got close, the beat of the music was loud and clear. Cecilia did not try to control her enthusiasm. She started dancing right there in the street, and her dance was like the booty dance I hated to see my granddaughters do.

Lawrence had a weird look on his face that I could not interpret. But when he said, "You go, girl. Show 'em what you're working with," I began to understand.

She danced us right up to the door, and when we entered, she let out a loud Haitian chant that got the attention of everybody in the club. She went right to the dance floor and put on a show that bordered on x-rated. She was popping and gyrating all over the floor. The beat of the music was like a stimulant, and the stronger the beat, the more repulsive her dance moves became. Several guys tried to join her, but each time she put up a strong sign by extending her arm, palm facing forward, as if to say, "Stop. This is my show," while her body kept twerking and working it out.

I don't know exactly what she thought was going to happen when she suggested I wear flat shoes because there was no way I could even attempt to dance to the beat of this music. I wasn't sure what kind of music it was, but I knew it was not reggae; it was much too fast. Finally, Cecilia took a bow and came off the dance floor to thunderous applause and accolades from the deejay.

"That's how we do it in Haiti," the deejay said in his thick Haitian accent. "You represented, my sista; you represented Haiti! Your table can drink all you want; it's on the house."

"Now we party," Cecilia stated proudly as she leaned over and gave Lawrence a kiss on the cheek. "Karah, you like?" Sweat was dripping from every part of her body.

"I loved it; you are amazing."

"Now I teach you. We dance together—so much fun and very healthy."

"Girl, I don't think so. This body has seen its best dancing days. Now I take it nice and slow." But then I thought that dancing with other retirees was pretty special.

"I can teach you some moves," she insisted. "I taught Lawrence, right, ba?"

"Well, you tried, and I can shake my groove thang a little but not like my baby. She always steals the show, so nobody even notices me."

We laugh and drank until after midnight. Cecilia drank spiced rum with Diet Coke, and I sipped on my French 75. Lawrence chose beer, which kept him going to the bathroom. During one of his trips, the deejay came down and introduced himself.

"Ladies, are you enjoying yourselves?" he asked in his sexy accent.

"Yes, thank you," Cecilia replied. I just smiled and nodded.

"My name is Kevin—DJ Clash, around here."

"My name is Cecilia, and this is my friend Karah. And this"—she nodded toward Lawrence, who had just returned to the table—"is the love of my life, Lawrence."

Lawrence asked Kevin to join us, and he did. He and Cecilia were both from Port-au-Prince and shared stories of their homeland. It was intriguing and informative because I knew very little about Haiti. Before Kevin returned to the deejay booth to close the night, he asked if he could buy us breakfast nearby. Lawrence was yawning repeatedly, but we thought it was a great idea.

The next night, at a different club, Cecilia did the same thing and received the same results—drinks for the table. This girl was a performer and was paid well for her skills. For the next few days, I learned that Cecilia was a girl gone wild. She had no limits to what she thought was fun, and she had a man who loved every moment of it. Some of her suggestions were too much for me. I didn't even try to attempt those moves, not even when she slowed down to teach me. Even though none of my offspring was watching or commenting on my every move, there was only so much letting loose I could do. I always would maintain some level of control. Besides, where in the world would I have the need for such dirty dancing? I loved to dance, but I wanted to learn different styles of dance. I was fascinated by Latin dances, ballroom dance, and stepping. I'd even seen some Haitian dance moves that were elegant and classy, but there was simply no need for Cecilia's wretched moves, and I quickly stopped her from even asking me.

Remarkably, however, they were able to convince me to go into a gentlemen's club. I had never been inside one, but if she suggested accompanying her man, I figured it couldn't be all bad. Besides, I was all for experiencing new things. I just hoped she didn't get on that pole.

I asked Cecilia what to wear; she said it was formal.

"There will be money in this place," she explained. "Lawrence brought me there once, and ever since, I am the one who insists on going."

Hm, I thought as I waited for them to finish dressing in my bedroom. I was anxious to look through my closet. When Cecilia came out of the room in a sassy red mini and gold accessories, it was impressive. I had never seen her in heels, and she looked very elegant. Lawrence was wearing a beige linen suit and a caramel-colored hat and shoes. He actually looked like he was from Columbia. They truly complemented each other, and I wondered briefly if I should have given Lawrence a chance. I quickly dismissed that thought because I never felt a spark for him, not even in my loneliest moments.

Following their lead on the attire, I wore a gray silk dress with sequins and with gray sling-backs and a sequined clutch bag. I looked forward to spending this evening with them.

The club was too far to walk, so Lawrence drove. He had an older model Tahoe, but it was in mint condition. It was obvious that he took more interest in his vehicles than his house.

Maybe Cecilia will encourage him to replace that worn-out furniture in his living room, I thought as we drove to the club. I sat in the centered of the back seat and could see each of them clearly. I noticed Lawrence mouth something as he looked over at Cecilia. In response, she said, "I love you too, baby."

Lawrence drove slowly through the parking lot. "It doesn't look that busy tonight, ladies."

"Well, it's kind of early," I said.

"No, it's Sunday, and that's always a slow night," Lawrence replied. "It may be perfect for you, Karah, since it's your first time. It can get sort of rowdy on Friday and Saturday nights. The guys are much younger and a lot less dignified. But these bouncers don't play around. You will be asked to leave if you act too crazy. And if asked, please don't hesitate, or you'll get pounced on."

When we entered, it was nothing like I expected. The music was soft, the décor was elegant, and I did not see any poles.

"Let's go upstairs to my favorite spot," Cecilia suggested.

"By all means," Lawrence responded.

We walked up a few steps—and I saw my first pole. It was straight ahead, and it looked like someone was about to do something.

"Oh good, we're just in time," Cecilia said. "Karah, these girls are the best. Elite pole dancers; they always amaze me."

Lawrence led us to a table close to the stage; he was a complete gentleman as he seated us and summoned the waitress. "The usual, ladies?" he asked.

"Yes," we each replied.

The stage lights dimmed, and the dancer gracefully appeared. She turned slightly to her left, gripping the pole with her left hand. She looked out at the audience and gave a gentle nod. The music started to play. I couldn't identify it, but it sounded like ... opera? *No way!* I thought. It certainly was opera, and it was the only kind of music that could accommodate this level of dance. As soon as her musical note prompted her, she began her routine, and with a long reach, her right hand was halfway up the pole. Supported only with her hands, her body was spread-eagled in midair. Her body looked like a sculpture, with every detail magnified by ten. She held her pose beyond expected limits and did a free-fall halfway down the pole. The crowd gasped, and my heart pounded as she stopped abruptly and released her right hand. Her feet gently reconnected with the floor as she danced a few sultry moves gracefully around the pole.

Once again, both hands were on the pole, and she climbed feverishly to the top. Her body was flipping and swirling and twirling continuously with rhythmic control. At times she flopped like a ragdoll and then was as rigid as a figurine. From the top of the pole, she flipped, and her body was straight as an arrow, parallel to the pole. Her feet stretched up toward the ceiling, with her head and eyes watching the audience. Her athleticism was phenomenal. Inch by exaggerated inch, hand over hand, she walked down the entire length of the pole, and her dismount ended in the splits. She sprang to her feet, took a bow, and sashayed away with attitude, muscles bulging. She clearly was a body sculptor, ballerina, and pole dancer, all wrapped in one. She was an athlete, and as with other athletes, her performance reflected her dedication and commitment to perfecting her skills. Although her title was "pole dancer," no money was tossed, and there was no vulgar language or sexual innuendo. No, this was an artist, and her performance was impeccable.

15

Emotional Roller Coaster

Lawrence and Cecilia left the next day, and I felt extremely lonely. I'd enjoyed their company and now felt empty. I tried to get back in my routine, but something had changed. All the exposure to dance and entertainment ignited my creativity, but I had just finished my final draft, and I wasn't ready to start a new book. I always liked to review the final project so I could implement any necessary changes. After all, my writing was a work in progress. It was like a writing class, and each book represented a promotion to the next level. Therefore, I could not get ahead of myself. I had to wait for the latest book to be released.

In my head, I could still hear the music of the performance at the gentlemen's club. I did a little research and found that the performer we had watched was a ballet dancer and had recently won a pole-dance competition in Canada. She was very inspirational, and I yearned for more—not necessarily more pole dancing but more of the art in general. I wanted to see a musical or stage play or even ballet.

I went to the Dr. Phillips Performing Arts Center website and reviewed the calendar. Several events interested me, so I bought tickets and attended several over the next few months. I always dressed formal for these events because it just felt right. During the intermission of one of the musicals, I was approached by a gentleman named Lambert. He and I quickly became very cordial with each other and discussed our opinions of the musical. He then asked if I would be attending another event in the future.

"I have a ticket to *Rage* next week—the matinee," I said.

"If I buy a ticket, could we sit together?"

I didn't see any problem with that suggestion, so I agreed.

The day of the play, Lambert was waiting for me in the lobby, and we enjoyed the play together. Afterward, it was early evening, and he suggested we go to the steakhouse across the street for dinner. He said he had not been there before, but Ted had taken me there, so I told Lambert it was very nice. We enjoyed the evening together. He walked me home, and it appeared to be the beginning of an exciting new friendship.

After about a month, Lambert and I had made progress with our relationship. He had a lot of qualities I admired, and I think he felt the same about me. Of course, we both loved the arts, and everything we had in common seemed connected to that.

We also liked to work out and often did so together. We admired healthy bodies—each other's in particular. We both enjoyed various types of music, and one of us often mentioned to the other something we liked. We also loved to dance and became a familiar pair around town. I'd call him up and ask if he wanted to go get coffee or a meal, and we'd usually meet outside or at the restaurant of choice. I had not invited him to my apartment, and he hadn't asked. But we walked and talked about everything.

Lambert had lived in Michigan most of his life and was retired from Ford Motor Company. He'd moved to Florida ten years ago because it was more economical and because he "just got tired of the cold weather." Most of his family still lived in Detroit, but he had a daughter who lived near Jacksonville.

I told him about Lawrence and Cecilia, who lived in Savannah, and suggested that we take a trip in the future. We both had crossover vehicles and discussed our respect for the road. We considered ourselves to be good drivers. This was like music to my ears. I usually didn't feel comfortable unless I was behind the wheel because of my lack of trust and the fact that many people I had traveled with simply were not good drivers. Riding close to someone's bumper or messing with the music, or just changing lanes without signaling drove me up the wall. My husband had loved to ride in the passing lane, and if he was driving the speed limit, he did not care who rode his bumper; he would not get over. That was the cause of many arguments, may God rest his soul.

Despite all Lambert and I had in common, we were still very cautious. Sometimes our measured show of affection was obvious. Once, we had gone to dinner and were walking along Eola Lake. He told me how much he enjoyed my company and that he treasured our friendship. I told him I felt the same way.

"It's not every day I meet women I like," he said, "so this is very special."

here was a long pause, and I prompted him to continue.

"Well, I don't want you to take this out of context, but I just wanted to show my appreciation, so I got you something as a token of our friendship."

His hand was trembling when he handed me a small jewelry box.

I searched for a quick reply. "Oh, you shouldn't have." I opened it and saw a gold bracelet made of connecting hearts. I was so excited, but I just said, "How sweet. Thank you!" I said and gave him a friendly hug.

"It's not a lot, but I wanted you to have it. I don't expect you to wear it all the time."

"I'll treasure it always."

When I got home I put it on and just marveled at it. What did it mean? Was he the one? I knew without a doubt that things were getting deep for me after a conversation with Ted. He wanted to know when he could come down and take me out for dinner and a show. I told him I wasn't sure and that I'd have to call him back. The fact of the matter was, I didn't want him to come. I wanted to spend my time with Lambert, and I didn't want Lambert to see Ted and get the wrong idea and become discouraged. I knew my plan was to date, and there was no reason to stop seeing my friends. But I liked Lambert, and I just wanted to spend my time with him now.

We started to get out more and went to all the theme parks in the area. We both loved the water, so we went to the beach. We had lunch in the park and shared more and more of ourselves. We had visited several churches and planned to visit more. One day we were lying on the beach, facing each other as we talked.

Suddenly, his appearance seemed to change. His mouth was sexy. His teeth were a brilliant white, and when he laughed, I felt so free. I looked into his eyes, and the sun's rays made the brown look like glitter. *This man is honest and true and certainly could be the man for me,* I thought. For the first time in almost two months and after many unheeded opportunities, I kissed him passionately on the mouth. Pulling me closer, he kissed me right back, and at that moment, under the open skies, we captured each other's hearts.

From that day forward, Lambert and I openly expressed our affection for each other. We were headed to church the next Sunday morning, and Lambert was enthusiastically talking about our relationship as he drove. He often said he adored me and wanted to take care of me, but now he was talking about our families.

"Karah we can do so many things together. We can travel to Alabama and Michigan to see our relatives. My family is going to love you. I can't wait for you to meet them. Mama is almost ninety, and she is always asking when I'm going to find a wife—someone to take care of me. I am her baby boy, you know."

I thought about my mama and tears filled my eyes. She would have been so happy to meet Lambert. He was such a good man, and I wished she could have seen me happy, with a good, strong man in my life. *Oh, Mama,* I thought. My face crumpled, and tears streamed from my eyes.

Lambert was calling my name. "Karah, honey, did you hear me?"

I was crying so hard I didn't want to hold my head up. I felt the car jerk when he pulled off at the next exit and drove to a service station and parked. He came around to my side of the car and opened the door, squeezing onto the seat with me.

My goodness, I thought.

"What's wrong, baby? Are you sick?"

"No, I'm sorry. I was just thinking about my mama."

"Oh, baby, I'm so sorry. That was so inconsiderate of me. Please forgive me."

"No, don't blame yourself. I still have these moments sometimes."

"I love you, and I have to be aware of the things that upset you and not just blurt things out." He wiped my face with a tissue. "Now look at you—your makeup is everywhere."

"You ... love me?" I said.

He stopped, as if he was taken by surprise. Then, looking deeply into my eyes, he said it again. "Yes, I love you, Karah. I love you very much." I just smiled. "You're my baby. You make me so very happy." He just held me close until the awkward seating got too uncomfortable. He stood up and said, "Now ... what about church?"

"I'm sure church has started already, and I'm really not up to it now. Can we just go back? We can come next Sunday."

"Sure, precious, whatever you prefer."

"I just need to lie down for a while."

Once we got back, Lambert accompanied me to my apartment. He still hadn't been there; I always met him in the lobby. But we had been seeing each other for two months, and on this day, neither of us could say goodbye.

He was a real gentleman, and he made sure I was comfortable. He joined me on the couch—no music, no television, just totally quiet. I could feel his heartbeat as I cuddled up close to his chest. I felt safe and secure as he gently stroked my face.

"Just let me love you, Karah," he whispered softly. "I know your life has not been so kind. You've had to be so strong. Now God has put us together so I can take care of you. You're my princess; we can take care of each other, love each other, and live the rest of our lives together. I'm not here to hurt or deceive you, baby. I want to be your mate through all things. I want to be the one you call whenever you need anything. I want to be the one you talk to about anything on your mind. I want to dance with you, sing with you, and cry with you. I want to make you my wife. Just let me show you." He sat up quickly and knelt in front of me.

He just gazed into my eyes. It felt kind of odd.

"What? What are you thinking?" I asked.

After a long pause, he said, "Us, baby, us—you and me. I don't want to do anything to jeopardize what we have. How are you? Are you feeling better?"

"Yes, I'm okay now."

"I tell you what—let's go out and grab a bite to eat and get some fresh air."

"Sure, that sounds good. I am hungry."

We had lunch and returned early. This time I turned on the music and opened a bottle of wine. We danced and sang and enjoyed the evening. It was getting late, but I did not want him to leave me.

"I don't want to be alone tonight," I told him. "Please stay."

He agreed without hesitation. I made sure he was comfortable. Then I went into the bathroom. I meticulously went through my entire beauty ritual. I took a long bubble bath and lavished every inch of my body in a sweet-scented body lotion. After cleansing my face, I reapplied my mascara and lipstick. I put on sexy silk pajamas. When I walked out to Lambert, he was asleep. I eased over and attempted to kiss him on the cheek.

He grabbed me roughly. It frightened me.

"Hey, *what are you doing*?" I squealed.

"Oh, babe." He released me. "Don't sneak up on me like that."

I was speechless; I knew that reaction. Shocked, I shouted, "Lambert!" Then I just froze; flashbacks were filling in pieces of a puzzle. I'd seen some questionable actions and odd reactions that had concerned me before. This time I'd seen something familiar.

"Lambert, are you a veteran?" I asked, my gaze intense.

"What does that matter?" he asked.

"It matters a lot to me. Please answer me. Are you a veteran?"

"Yes, I went to Nam for a brief tour."

"Why didn't you tell me?" I asked without blinking an eye.

"Karah, it's not important. That had nothing to do with my reaction. You just scared me."

"No, you should have told me. Please leave."

"What? You can't be serious."

"Oh, I'm very serious. Leave now, please!"

"No, let's talk."

"Not now, not now. Please go. Don't make me ask you again."

"Fine!" he replied, and he walked out the door.

Lambert called me repeatedly in the days that followed, and each time I told him I didn't want to talk. *How could this be possible?* I asked myself. Day after day, I searched my mind for any logical reason but could find nothing. I could not think of one reasonable explanation, and I need one badly.

Finally, I agreed to meet Lambert in the park. When he approached me, he was almost unrecognizable. He hadn't shaved, and his eyes were bloodshot. His clothes were wrinkled, and he smelled of alcohol. Through unmanageable tears, he told me he was a veteran and had been to Vietnam. He said he had a problem with alcohol and was once homeless. The Veterans Administration put him through a program and diagnosed him with post-traumatic stress disorder.

"Coming to this area was a part of my treatment program," he explained.

I was disappointed and heartbroken. "I'm a veteran," I reminded him. "I have been to war, but I told you that from the beginning. Even then, you never mentioned a word about being a veteran. Why? It's the same as not telling me you'd been married or had children. How could you leave those things out when you're trying to get to know someone?" I'm sure he felt mentioning his time in Nam would open the door to events he preferred to forget, but I felt it was the wrong thing to do. "We have spent too much quality time together for you not to have mentioned such vital information."

He kept apologizing and insisting that it would never happen again.

I shook my head sadly. "Things will never be the same," I said. Then I said goodbye and walked away.

I was still disappointed and heartbroken after the situation with Lambert, and I still missed him a lot. Nevertheless, moving on was most important, so I focused on the positive and pushed pass all other possibilities.

Lambert still lived near me, and I would see him in the city from time to time. Each encounter led to a long discussion about how we could work things out. I repeatedly made it clear that this was irreconcilable. His persistence eventually became annoying—sometimes frightening.

Early one morning when I walked out of my building, there he was, waiting for me. I just kept walking. He grabbed me by my arm. As I snatched it away, I made it clear that I was not going to be harassed. My apartment building was monitored twenty-four/seven, and I usually felt safe and secure. Immediately after that encounter, however, I felt it necessary to emphasize to management that no one was to have access to my apartment unless they were with me or their name was on the visitors log. I refused to allow his deception to steal my joy.

Lambert had made a bad decision by not telling me, and I was not going to make any excuses for him. Still, I couldn't understand how I could get it so wrong. It had felt so real, so spiritual. All I could do was pray for peace.

16

Big Pretty Picture Coming into View

Ted was still calling, and so was Lawrence. They both wanted to visit, but I was not in the mood. I missed my family, and I started to think a lot about going home. I'd told them the last time I left that I'd be gone at least a year before I returned, unless there was an emergency. It had been about nine months, so I forced myself to resist the temptation. I spent more time working out and going to fine-art presentations.

One Saturday morning my phone rang; it was my editor.

"Karah, are you sitting down?"

"No, should I be?"

"Yes, ma'am, you are not going to believe this."

"Go on. I need some good news."

"Your book is a hit!"

"*What?*"

"Yes, all the editors love it, and we want to feature it on our website."

"Wonderful!" I replied.

"Karah, your sales are going to go through the roof, and of course that means more money for all involved."

"That is great news! Now I can start on my next book."

"Well yeah, but what about marketing the four you have? Are you ready to implement your plans?"

"I'm not sure. Since I've moved to Orlando, my plans will need to be adjusted. I will not have the support of the colleges I attended, but I can still do the billboards. I live in the downtown area, and there is a library and a fine arts center. Maybe I can take advantage of that. I just haven't given it much thought. Can we talk about it later?"

"Sure, I'll give you a call in about a week."

I didn't share his level of enthusiasm. My writing was obviously improving, and that was great. But for me, it wasn't just about book sales. I wanted to be recognized for the stories I told. Most of my writing was based on real events, and the power of God was always present. That is what I wanted to capture. That is what I wanted readers to come away with. Still, I knew I should be more excited.

Something was wrong. I could feel my depression slipping in. If I allowed that to happen, it wouldn't matter where I lived or how many books I had on the best-seller list. Life would turn dark. I had to go, to get out and feel the sun on my face. I had to breathe fresh air. I had to remind myself from where I had come and where I was trying to go.

Keep pushing; be the best you possible, I told myself. *Forget about Lambert. You forgot about K. C., and you knew him for eighteen beautiful months.*

I had been with my husband for over ten years, and I was able to find my joy again after both of those loses, and I would again. Right now, however, I felt like I once again was trying to climb, and I couldn't get a grip. Once again, I felt that I was in a place where I could get caught in a web.

After wallowing in self-pity for a while, I had to remind myself that God was still on the throne. He had guided and directed me all my life, and he would again. I now had everything I had dreamed of, but I still wasn't happy. That was a problem. I had to reevaluate what it was all about. Was it all about my significant other? When Lambert and I were together, I was fine. Our relationship was all that had changed recently, and I felt lost. Maybe my emotions were all over the place because I didn't have my mate. Well, if that was the case, God was the answer. I did not want to choose or be chosen unless it was blessed by God. I only wanted the man God selected for me—my soul mate.

It was the fall season, and the days were getting shorter. I still walked for exercise and for pleasure, but this morning I was jogging. I had passed the coffee shop and then turned the corner by the bookstore—and I could not believe my eyes. According to the signs in the window, my book was featured in the bookstore in the Local Authors section. I went inside, and sure enough—there it was on the shelves. I introduced myself to the manager and asked how it came about.

"One of the editors called me and told me you had recently moved to the area and needed to establish yourself as an author. He also said that you needed help with marketing your books, so I agreed to feature the latest one. It's been on the shelves a few days now and is selling quite well. When can we discuss the details of your book signing? We need to set a date and venue before we can do the advertising. People come from all over the state for book-signing events. They like to get up close and personal with a rising new artist. I'm usually here nine to five, Monday and Tuesday. Come by, and let's talk soon."

"Oh, I sure will."

We made plans to have the book signing on Veteran's Day. She thought that would generate a lot of publicity and sales. I liked the idea of focusing on the veterans; that meant a lot to me. Now, because of all the publicity, I was the town celebrity. When people recognized me, they always insisted on buying me something—coffee or drinks. I would talk with them and answer their questions. Most people wanted to know how to get started as a writer, more so than about the contents of the books.

Back home, after each of my books was released, I had small signing events at my house. The question-and-answer session could get sort of crazy. I had three books on the market, and people would randomly ask me about the contents of any of them. Sometimes my recollection wasn't so great, and I would cleverly pass the question to the other people in the room. I was always impressed with the amount of detail people knew. They called the characters by name and wanted to know if they would be written back into stories in the future. They often asked about Dominique, my sister in the stories, and Tynisha, my daughter in the stories, who was so mischievous that one time someone yelled, "Tynisha should still be on punishment!"

We had two random book signings at the library, and Lawrence and Cecilia came down for both. Lambert also came to one of the events and bought a book. He looked at me with such disappointment as he asked me to sign "love always." I obliged him and moved on to the next person. I was not a cold-hearted person, but I refused to adjust and help people fit into my life. Just be open and honest; that was all I asked. I made that clear from the start because I knew what my response would be to such foolishness, and it would be quick and decisive. That's just the way it was with me, and I didn't care how much it hurt. I only wanted the person God chose for me, and that person would reveal all, and we would not begin our relationship based on lies.

The next book signing was scheduled for November 11, Veteran's Day, at the Dr. Phillips Performing Arts Center. It was to last from eleven in the morning until four. The local news outfits would be there, and there would be a question-and-answer session for fifteen minutes at the end of every hour.

Naomi and Shelly flew in the day before, so they were there to help me get ready. All my children were driving down that morning. I wouldn't be calm until they all got there. Shelly did my makeup, and it was perfect. She also did her mom's, whose behavior reminded me of my first time getting lashes.

"Mom, stay still," she kept repeating.

"I'm trying; you know I can't tolerate people being in my face."

"Damn, that must be a military thing," I said before telling them my lash story.

It was wonderful having my two favorite girls with me as I got ready for my big event. I knew their love for me was genuine, and they were going to make sure I looked my best.

We agreed on a short sparkling silver dress and long silver earrings with three fuchsia stones and a necklace to match. Naomi bought me a beautiful waterfall ring to wear on the index finger of my signing hand. Shelly gave me a several refillable signing pens with backup ink cartridges. Fuchsia was my favorite color, and it matched the book cover perfectly. I wanted everything to look elegant. This would be the largest book event I'd ever hosted, and I did not want things to be downplayed.

As soon as we arrived at the fine arts building, I had a hot flash. I felt hot and nauseated.

"Have them turn the air up, please," I said.

"You okay, girlie?" Naomi asked.

"Yeah, just let me sit here for a minute."

"Nerves, girl; those are your nerves. Just think positive. Think about being on the beach in Hawaii. Just don't think about Koko Head!"

We all laughed and went inside

"Look at you, girl!" Naomi said as we looked at my portrait. "You look beautiful!"

"Yes, Auntie, you look so young."

"Yes, all those air-brushing techniques really work."

A few guests began to arrive as we mingled and talked among ourselves. The décor was everything I'd asked for. Fuchsia brightened up the entire room.

"Oh, my God, look at my warrior princess!" I heard Kimberly say.

"Oh, look at Grandma! She's so pretty," said one of my grandkids.

"Those are my children!" I said to Naomi and Shelly. "Prepare to be amazed."

I introduced everyone and got them seated before my signing started.

"Karah, my goodness. They all look alike; I mean, every one of them," Naomi said with amazement.

"Be nice," I said to my children. "I'll see y'all soon. Remember to purchase one of the books so I can sign it for you."

"I'm getting all four of them, girl, so I'll be one of the first for you to sign," Naomi said.

"Well, you'd better come on; that line is already getting long."

I signed books for the first hour. The place was full of people getting their books signed, and then they sat and waited for the question-and-answer session to begin. After I signed the last book, I grabbed my bottled water. I knew this could be a long process. People could ask questions about any of the books, so I had to be ready. They had already received numbers to make the process go faster and to be fair.

"Who has number one?" I asked.

A lady raised her hand. "I just want to know if you plan to write a sequel to *Boots to Stilettos*."

"No, actually, *Boots to Stilettos* is the last of a three-book series." She thanked me, and I called the next number. "Number two?"

Another woman raised her hand. "I just wanted to make a comment about *Vengeance Is Mine*."

"Yes, go ahead."

"Well, I just thought you could have used a better choice of words."

Chuckles were sprinkled throughout the audience.

"Well, I did have a limited vocabulary, and I decided not to have that modified by the editors. I hope that in the following books, you can see an improvement, and in the future, I hope I can look back and say, 'Wow, I can't believe I used to write so poorly.'"

Everyone laughed. A few more questions were asked, and then it was back to the book signing. The day went well. We stopped for lunch around noon—just chips and sandwiches in the reception area for thirty minutes—and then it was back to the signing. The next few Q&A sessions went well, but after the last session, someone asked me to read a poem. One poem led to another, so I spent that Q&A session reading poetry. I was exhausted.

Finally, it was the last signing hour, so I smiled graciously and greeted each person as if he or she was the first person of the day. Then came the final Q&A, and as soon as I heard the first question, my demeanor changed. This was uncomfortable territory for me, and it had been avoided all night.

"I just want to know why you didn't take your flight to visit K. C."

"Well, as I tried to explain in the book, I didn't want to commit to K. C., to a ready-made family. Next question?"

I heard the same voice again, this time closer to me. "I always thought that was a poor excuse."

Now who's this wise ass? I thought. *Sounds like Dewayne.* I wanted to tell him to stop, but the room was crowded, and I stayed professional.

"Well, actually, sir, that decision was made with K. C.'s best interest in mind. Next question?"

Again, I heard the same voice. "If you had it to do all over, would you take the flight?"

"Well, it sounds like some of my readers think I should have."

People started laughing, then clapping and clapping.

Oh, my God, I thought, *are they really clapping in response to that?*

Again, that voice chimed in. "Well, Ms. Karah Woodard, I think you should make it right."

The voice sounded too familiar. I stood up and looked out over the audience—and oh, my God; it was Keith Covington, aka K. C., the love of my life. Neither of us said another word. I heard Kimberly say, "That's K. C."

He walked all the way up to the signing table and looked right into my eyes, reached across the table, and grabbed my hands. "You know I wouldn't miss this for the world," he said softly.

Before closing the event, I gave a special thank-you to all the veterans in the room and around the world. The book signing event was a success, and I was surrounded by family and friends. I introduced everyone to K. C., who was very gracious as they bombarded him with questions. He had a morning flight scheduled for the following day, so I took that opportunity to usher him away for dinner. Lawrence and Cecilia were heading back home, so we said our goodbyes. Everyone else was staying for adventures in Orlando the following day.

K. C. and I had dinner together and caught up on each other's lives. I was curious about how he found out, and he just said, "I have my connections."

Our lives were good. We were both happy and expressed no desire to replay the past. It was very clear that things were just as they should be. We laughed and talked as we walked around the city, each commenting on how much it reminded us of Germany. I took him to my favorite jazz bar, and he loved it. After hours of laughing and talking, it was time to say goodbye, and my heart ached. He walked me to my apartment and gave me a long, powerful hug.

"Take care of yourself, Karah," he whispered in my ear, grabbing hold of both my hands.

All I could say was, "You take care, and thank you for being here."

I was in a trance as I made my way upstairs. Did the love of my life just walk in and back out of my life, or was I dreaming? Stepping over collapsed bodies throughout the living room, I found my way out onto the balcony. I curled up on my chaise lounge and relaxed as I replayed the events of this remarkable evening.

I awoke to the beautiful sounds of morning, and a gentle smile came to my face. The sun rising over the lake, a cool breeze blowing, birds chirping, airplanes flying—it all signified new beginnings. I was reminded of God's amazing presence in my life. All the things I'd seen and experienced were orchestrated by almighty God. He ordered my steps, guided my thoughts, gave me wisdom and strength. Most importantly, I had finally learned to rest in God's peace. He was in control of my life, and he made no mistakes. I looked forward to the amazing things he had planned for my future.

"All is well, Mama," I said. "All is well!"

Printed in the United States
By Bookmasters